CW01501445

Brian McHarg was born in Reading, England in 1949. Together with his second wife Lesley, they have five children and eleven grandchildren. After retiring as a Managing Director of an electronics company in 2005, he moved to Lanzarote in the Canary Islands. It was during the pandemic that, together with the assistance of Lesley, he began writing in earnest.

During that period, he also published three small illustrated children's books in his *Grandfather's Chest* series. This novel, however, is his first full length thriller.

I dedicate this book to my late mother, May McHarg, who, as an English teacher, was passionate about the language. She inspired that in me too and ensured I knew my grammar and used English correctly!

Brian McHarg

PATHWAYS

AUSTIN MACAULEY PUBLISHERS

LONDON * CAMBRIDGE * NEW YORK * SHARJAH

Copyright © Brian McHarg 2025

The right of Brian McHarg to be identified as author of this work has been asserted by the author in accordance with sections 77 and 78 of the Copyright, Designs and Patents Act 1988.

All rights reserved. No part of this publication may be reproduced, stored in a retrieval system, or transmitted in any form or by any means, electronic, mechanical, photocopying, recording, or otherwise, without the prior permission of the publishers.

Any person who commits any unauthorised act in relation to this publication may be liable to criminal prosecution and civil claims for damages.

This is a work of fiction. Names, characters, businesses, places, events, locales, and incidents are either the products of the author's imagination or used in a fictitious manner. Any resemblance to actual persons, living or dead, or actual events is purely coincidental.

A CIP catalogue record for this title is available from the British Library.

ISBN 9781035879458 (Paperback)
ISBN 9781035879465 (ePub e-book)

www.austinmacauley.com

First Published 2025
Austin Macauley Publishers Ltd®
1 Canada Square
Canary Wharf
London
E14 5AA

I would like to thank my wife's endless patience when I was glued to a laptop for about a year writing this book. She also drove me on when I was close to giving up. Several key twists in the book were her ideas.

Also, thanks to other family members who constantly encouraged me to complete it.

Each had their reason…

There were thirteen of them, from all walks of life. They didn't know each other but all had a common need—they were each desperate to escape the UK. Would they all succeed? A rollercoaster of a ride awaited them all, and finally, a surprise destination for some. A place where they would be forced to face a mission together—a most difficult and dangerous one.

Chapter 1

Heathrow was heaving as usual. A new flight was arriving and another departing almost every minute. One could only marvel at how it all seemed to run so smoothly; well, usually anyway. The departure lounge at Gate A16 was no different from the other sixty-five at this newest international terminal, number 5. It was packed to capacity with no room to sit anywhere. The tannoy echoed, in its usual distorted and abrupt manner, "Will all passengers departing on Flight BA0285 to San Francisco please go immediately to gate A16, where this flight is now ready for boarding."

Peter Andrews was already there. He wanted to get away as quickly as he could. He was far from certain that he would achieve this at all and he wasn't the only one. This was a routine daily flight for British Airways, but for some, this flight was to be far from normal. There were two hundred and thirty-five people waiting to board this Boeing 777–300 on its eleven-hour flight to San Francisco.

For a few, this was not their final destination, although they didn't yet know exactly where it would be. All they did know was that they were all attempting to escape the UK for a new life.

At the final gate, boarding passes were being checked against the infallible Heathrow Computer System. A system that sometimes was as slow as an outdated home computer! Peter was probably not alone in being nervous. Would he get away? any record of his pending court appearance? It was one he clearly did not plan to attend…

Sitting next to him in the lounge was an elderly woman of Asian appearance, who also seemed nervous. Maybe more so than him. He asked her, "Have you been to San Francisco before?"

"No," she replied. "Not only have I never been there before, but this is my first plane flight!"

"Don't be nervous. I have flown scores of times, always safe and uneventful."

She replied, "I am trying to relax, but it isn't easy! My son is getting married in San Jose next week and I am trying to just think about that." She went on to tell Peter that her son worked in a large hotel there. Now he understood her nervousness and confirmed that she wasn't 'one of us'. *Who were the others?* he wondered. The organiser, who always had been anonymous, had said there would also be others taking their escape on this flight.

He looked around the lounge. Everyone looked normal. No clues as to who the others were. They were all usual cross-section of men, women, and children; most of them heading to their sunshine destination. Peter noticed a middle-aged couple sitting opposite him, who certainly seemed somewhat agitated.

He could hear their nervous chatter. "I don't know why this is taking so long to get us boarding," the man said. "We are already over thirty minutes late."

"Don't worry," his partner replied. "They are just making the final checks on board and these things do take time." She sounded reassuring but was clearly nervous too. He later found out that these were Jayne and Alan, who were also part of the escape group. Finally, the call came for boarding. One by one, everyone passed through the final boarding pass check and entered the huge wide-bodied Boeing 777–300. A very new plane by the look of the carpets and the fresh seating.

Every time Peter took these long-haul flights, which he had done many times before, he found it intensely annoying that they made sure you entered at the front, getting a clear view of the privileged first-class passengers up front. There, they had wide leather-looking seats with enough legroom to lie back and sleep.

Glancing at this expensive luxury to his left, he was directed to the right, to move back with the other 'cattle-class' passengers. The only consolation he could muster in his head was to recollect the fare difference. It was more than four times the price to join the elite in comparative luxury. At the end of the day, they were on the same plane, going to the same destination and arriving at the same time.

He wouldn't worry about the seats, the legroom or the lack of complimentary gin and tonics! Peter was sitting in row 15, with a pre-booked window seat. He wanted to get some sleep on this eleven-hour flight; he thought he would need it for what was to follow. From many previous flight experiences, he knew that an aisle seat always meant being disturbed by someone needing a toilet visit. He settled down, opened up the in-flight magazine, and tried to relax.

In seat 17C, just a few rows behind him was Joanna Crawley. She too was far from relaxed. She also wondered who else sitting around her was sharing this final journey. She too had no idea where she was going. This really was unsettling her. She had been a very successful model until the threat of a scandal. How was he have to have known that MI6 was monitoring her relationship with that politician?

How was she to have known he would die under such mysterious and suspicious circumstances? How was she to have known that she had become the prime suspect in his untimely death? She had nothing to do with it of course, but it did, however, look most suspicious. Joanna contacted a website called Pathways which boasted UK escapes. It was an extensive website. She quickly became aware, however, that the costs of taking the escape they offered were high and also that the destination was held in mystery. Both concerned her considerably. She, however, weighed these things against the scandal she would surely face if she stayed much longer. They seemed to offer the solution to her dilemma.

She again looked around her, wondering who else was on this one-way excursion to a new future. She too had been told there would be others. She secretly hoped there would be a future partner for her. Sex had always been a big part of her life and she didn't feel, at just twenty-six years of age, that she was quite yet ready to become celibate.

At the other side of the far aisle, in seat 17H, was a Chinese man. He was Wan Lung, a forty-seven-year-old businessman from Ealing, West London. He had successfully sold car entertainment systems through the Internet for about ten years. At first sight, there seemed to be nothing illegal about any of his business dealings and, during that time, he had amassed a bank balance of about $4.3 million…but there was a dangerous flaw in his dealings. He naively thought he had skilfully hidden everything from the Inland Revenue and had never paid any UK tax. All was going well until a local tax inspector took a close look at his business dealings and investigated them.

Many people seem to think they will not be found, but at least the larger fish seem to eventually get caught! He received a visit from two senior officials from the tax office early one morning. The questions were difficult; the responses even more so. They knew that he had paid no tax for many years and finally, they had caught up with him. Well, they would have done, had he not joined this expedition. It was thanks to his lawyer that he had managed to find this journey to freedom. He knew he would always be grateful to him for his help, although he complained to close friends that he felt it was rather expensive! (Strange how people with considerable wealth all too often seem to count the pennies!)

Jonathan Clarke never meant to hurt anyone. He had just been unfortunate. Sorry, bad introduction. He was in row 31. He was with his son, Michael.

Jonathan had been drinking in a West End bar after his fifty-third birthday party and was considerably worse for several large beers, brandies, and other cocktails that he later wished he'd never had. The argument with the youth with tattoos and piercings ended with a very badly injured youngster; one who should never have taken on a retired middleweight boxer! His injuries were so severe that the pending court case was likely to result in a custodial sentence. He enjoyed a comfortable lifestyle and enjoyed the time he spent with his son. Prison was something he could not possibly contemplate.

There had to be an alternative, he told his lawyer. Here is the first part of this connection; his lawyer was the same one who was in the process of assisting several others on this flight too. He had the contact needed.

In all, there were thirteen people on this busy flight who were making their way to a new life. All had their own reasons and needs. All had one thing in common; none had much choice. They were all on a one-way journey, but their destination was not going to be San Francisco; although only one of them yet knew where it was to be. That person was going to be key to the overall plan as we will shortly see. What was clear was that each had paid a great deal of money and each was equally keen to get away.

Chapter 2

Antonio Alcosta was born in Zacapa, a small town in the north-eastern region of Guatemala. It had a population of just two hundred and seventy thousand people. His was a humble farming family whose main interest was growing coffee beans.

They owned a plantation in the fertile Motagua Valley, just seventy-five kilometres from their family home. His father travelled there daily, leaving home at 6 am and rarely returning before 8 pm. His wife kept the accounts up-to-date. Payroll and all other costs, along with income, were methodically recorded. The success of the business was a tribute to their hard work and determination.

Guatemala gained independence from Spain in the 1820s. It had a long history of military regimes until it came under democratic rule in 1985. Today, it is largely a peaceful place to live.

Growing coffee beans was a lucrative business and most were exported. Agriculture in the area provided employment for forty per cent of its inhabitants. The agricultural resources of Guatemala were rich, with the lower Monagua Valley being amongst the best for producing coffee. Antonio's family exploited its resources to the full.

At just thirty-four years of age, he tragically lost both his father and mother to a house fire that ripped through their wooden home in the early hours one morning. They didn't stand a chance. Antonio, sleeping in a downstairs room at the rear of the house, managed to escape. The fire was caused by an exploding gas bottle in the kitchen.

He and his older brother, Carlos, continued to run the business as best they could for a few more years. However, he had little interest in it and spent much of his time on his passion for gambling at a small casino in the city. He was quite good at calculating odds and knew when to bet and when not to! He thoroughly enjoyed it, generally winning more than he lost. He never felt addicted in any way and always gambled responsibly with pre-decided limits.

Antonio had no interest in the coffee plantation and promptly opened discussions with his brother to buy him out. The negotiations with Carlos were difficult as he drove a very hard bargain. It was clear that he resented Antonio leaving him behind to run the business alone. In truth, the brothers had little in common and didn't have much time for each other. Separating was probably for the best for them both.

A financial deal was eventually agreed and Carlos bought Antonio's share of the plantation from him.

The money enabled Antonio to guarantee a loan to buy a small local casino. The money he gradually made surprisingly quickly paid off the outstanding bank loan. The casino was soon his. His other passion was music; he had it playing in virtually every room in the house and twenty-four hours a day in his casino!

It was this interest in music that enticed him into buying a new revolutionary portable music player, invented by a start-up company in Ireland, rather strangely called Apple!

This company had initially pioneered small office computers with a unique one that was a massive success. The brains behind Apple was its founder, Steve Jobs. He established the Irish plant in 1980 with a single manufacturing facility in Cork. They employed just sixty staff initially. In 2020, they celebrated forty years of operations with their huge Cork facility, then employing over six thousand people!

Their handheld player housed a small disc drive could hold several hundred music tracks, which could then be listened to through small headphones. Antonio was most impressed with this innovative player and used it daily wherever he went.

Apple held patents on this technology, which prevented it from being copied by others. He appreciated the leap in technology they had achieved and he recognised their potential. This persuaded him that they would make a good investment.

He enjoyed a gamble and thought the odds looked good for a profit. He was right; the company went from strength to strength and they eventually moved to 'Silicon Valley' in California to further tap into the technical expertise there.

It was home to a large number of start-up electronic companies which attracted some of the best expertise in this field.

His relatively modest investment in this company grew beyond his wildest dreams. It was his best gamble to date!

Eventually, he had sufficient funds to purchase a much larger casino right in the centre of the city.

This one produced good profits and was an exciting venture. He spent all his time now backwards and forwards between these two lucrative investments. They were so successful that he was able to buy a large house that he converted into a comfortable hotel. He named it Pathways.

This further added to his already substantial income. He was quickly becoming a multi-millionaire.

This hotel boasted eighteen bedrooms, all at a four-star level. Although each room was unique with varied styles, all included the same facilities.

It was at this hotel that he met Kokee Gonzalez. She was true to the meaning of her first name, which was 'an intelligent woman'.

She was a quiet private person who didn't show her feelings to others. She was of a slight build, had shoulder-length black hair, and was rather attractive. Kokee managed this busy hotel. Something she did most efficiently. Antonio had complete faith in her as she was scrupulously honest and an extremely hard worker.

After only fourteen months of working together, they fell in love and decided to marry. He proposed to her whilst they were away in Austria skiing. Being a romantic, he did it on Valentine's Day! She accepted and was thrilled to find a breakfast waiting with champagne and a table dressed with a dozen roses! Antonio had requested that all be red, but only six were available at the local florist, so an additional six yellow ones were substituted. He insisted there were the full dozen.

They spent the whole of that day planning every detail of their wedding day. The first thing they did was to list the fifteen people who were essential guests. They contacted them all, either by email or by telephone, giving them three proposed dates with the request that each agree to as many as possible. With one exception, they found a date that suited all these VIPs. So the wedding date was finally fixed for 28 July.

They then booked out their hotel to accommodate as many guests as possible using the few remaining rooms that were available. They booked their local registry office for the legal side of things. Neither of them was religious so that was all they wanted. That ceremony was to be attended by just Antonio's brother and a small handful of close friends to be witnesses. This had been Antonio's first contact with his brother since leaving him on the plantation alone.

Two marquees were ordered. A small one to serve as a venue for a blessing. This again was only for a small group and had a religious slant to it to appeal to those that way inclined. Then, a second far larger marquee for the grounds was also ordered. This was to include chandeliers and be decorated in light blue throughout. Tables and seating were to be included for at least one hundred guests.

There was also a full bar with two staff and a stage for music entertainers; yet to be decided upon.

An outside caterer was also booked and the meal choices were made. For a starter, they chose Kak'ik (turkey soup) followed by Chiles Rellenos (stuffed chile peppers). These were to be stuffed with pork and vegetables, served on a bed of tomato-based red sauce. Both very traditional local dishes. The chosen wines were of course all local. Despite having plenty of money and could, of course, have comfortably paid someone to manage their special day, they wanted to do everything themselves. They then planned and executed the entire day with military precision, every detail was thought of, right down to the small red petals on the tables! The brains behind the day and indeed her husband's ventures were Kokee's from now on.

They were very happy. Both agreed it was one of their happiest days when discussing it later.

They booked a week at the MGM Grand Hotel in Las Vegas for their honeymoon. Whilst, with some five thousand rooms, it was the biggest hotel in the world at that time, it got overtaken by several even larger ones in the years that followed.

Of course, Vegas was noted for its casinos and as a haunt for seasoned gamblers. This suited Antonio well with his considerable knowledge of the games and how they worked.

He was looking forward to seeing if he could win some money, but also to learn more about how to do so by watching others, many with far more experience than him. They took a direct flight to Las Vegas the day after the wedding.

After checking into their room, they made a beeline straight into the massive casino. They were both amazed at the sheer size of it! One of the first things he quickly noticed was that there were employees; mainly scantily dressed young women, serving free drinks, nibbles, and even cigarettes! It became obvious that this was a technique to encourage longer stays at the tables and more relaxed, bold, confident gamblers! This was something that clearly worked and he decided he would implement a similar policy at their casinos on his return.

Whilst Kokee and he spent much of their time sightseeing and taking in local attractions, they also spent a fair bit of time at the tables. That time was well spent, as they learnt many tricks to improve the odds of winning. All were perfectly legal; they just took time to study and learn.

One of the evenings they really enjoyed was seeing Tom Jones perform in their hotel. The venue consisted of a relatively small area with round tables. The theatre was wide, but not deep, so everyone was quite close to the stage and thereby had a great view of this legendary artist. Included in the $100 entry price was a bottle of champagne on each table. The performance was superb. They both agreed that Tom was one of the few pop music artists who had actually succeeded in improving over the years. Whilst they were too young to remember, they knew Tom was from South Wales in the UK.

Also that he had a massive hit in the early 60s with what became his signature trademark song, *It's Not Unusual*. Whenever anyone was born, all knew this tune. He, of course, performed it to perfection on this occasion; it was his opening song! Many others followed as he entertained everyone for almost two hours. Afterwards, he came off the stage and spoke to some people. Finally, their honeymoon stay at this lovely hotel came to an end and they packed their cases to return home. This was after they counted their money and calculated that, even after paying for their stay, they were taking home just over $5,000 more than they had brought with them. It had been a very successful honeymoon all round! It was certainly the holiday of a lifetime!

Chapter 3

In row 15, Peter couldn't relax. Whilst he had successfully got on this plane and felt he would probably get away, he didn't know what would be the final outcome of this journey. He thought back to how it had all begun.

He was born in Reading, Berkshire, a thriving southern town, in 1988. Reading was famous for three things beginning with 'b' he had always been told by his father: blooms, biscuits, and beer. To explain, they were Suttons Seeds, a producer of packet seeds for the garden; world-famous eventually. They were the blooms.

Then Huntley & Palmers, the biscuit manufacturer. Again, world-famous. He remembered a school trip around their factory in the town. He was amazed by the sheer scale of the biscuit output that exceeded ten thousand an hour. All boxed and shipped throughout the world. That was the biscuits.

Then, there was Symonds, the beer manufacturer, situated in the Basingstoke road on the outskirts of the town. They eventually became Courage and later were taken over by a brewery conglomerate.

He had enjoyed an impressive tour around their brewery with his staff on a night out one year.

He was particularly impressed that, because they were incensed at the huge water rates charged by the local authority, they sunk their own well to produce their beer! That struck him as a great enterprise! So that was the beer. The third famous 'b' for Reading.

He was born in a small part of the town on the outskirts called Earley. He always was puzzled that this area was called that, as he had always been taught that 'early' was spelt differently. His family were middle class, both parents being teachers.

His mother taught at a local primary school in Earley and his father was a senior lecturer at Twickenham College. He taught French and also German; being fluent in both. Peter recalled that when visiting Germany with his father on student exchange schemes, people found it hard to believe he was English as his German was so perfect!

Peter went to a boarding school in Wantage called King Alfred's. It was not a private school, although, for those that were boarders like himself, fees had to be paid by his parents for accommodation and food, etc.

It was an excellent school and he achieved good exam results. On leaving, he was lucky enough to achieve entry for an apprenticeship at a large electronics company in Bracknell, a nearby town. There, he climbed the ladder and was now on their board.

One morning, riding his 250cc Triumph motorbike from Reading to Bracknell, he made a reckless manoeuvre; he overtook three cars at once and hit a woman trying to cross the road with a small child in her arms. Both were killed instantly. He was relatively unscathed, but when the police appeared on the scene, he wished he had never been born.

Peter didn't realise at first how serious the incident was. It took time for it all to sink in. Both the woman and small child had suffered horrific injuries, both were pronounced dead at the scene. The police gave him a breath test, which he failed. He was promptly arrested and taken to Bracknell police station. There, he was given a blood test and an intensive interview, which resulted in a full written statement being produced. After being held for seven hours, he was formally charged with drunk driving and causing death by dangerous driving. A date for trial was fixed for two months hence and he was released on bail.

When he had taken a taxi back to his home, he went to his bedroom and thought about what had happened. The night before was largely to blame. He had stayed out late and drunk far too much alcohol at a local club. Consequently, when the morning came, and it was time to get ready for work, he struggled to keep to a timely schedule. He had left home late and was rushing to make up for lost time.

It was riding his powerful motorbike at high speed, with a hangover, that was the root cause of the terrible accident that ensued. He didn't know any lawyer to hire to represent him, so he phoned a good friend with experience in the profession. He recommended someone he thought would be good for him. Peter phoned him immediately and made an appointment for the following morning.

After a sleepless night, he dressed in his best suit and tie, along with a white shirt. He couldn't face breakfast, so just went straight to the lawyer's office in town by taxi. The taxi driver talked non-stop all the way. Clearly, he was in a far better frame of mind than Peter was! The lawyer's office was on the fourth floor of an eight-story building. On entering, he was a little concerned about how scruffy and small it was. He wondered if this was really a successful lawyer. He knew that was certainly what he needed!

Miles Parker had been a lawyer for twenty years and assured Peter that he had won far more cases than he had lost. This statement provided Peter with some much-needed encouragement. Peter slowly explained what had happened and the circumstances leading up to his subsequent arrest and charges. Miles listened patiently, saying nothing. When Peter finished, he stroked his chin thoughtfully.

Peter had been watching his expressions closely, looking for any reaction to his story. He couldn't fail to miss the frowns that were deep on his brow; he clearly didn't like the sound of any of it at all. He pulled no punches in telling Peter that he was facing very serious charges, ones that would certainly result in a custodial sentence. The length of which would be the only open question for the judge to decide.

It was established that Peter was previously of good character and, with the exception of a couple of parking tickets with a hire car, he had no previous record. This, Miles explained, would go in his favour, albeit only slightly. It was also clear that he had unknowingly ridden his motorbike still under the influence of alcohol from the night before. He had not deliberately committed a drunk driving offence. Nevertheless, he had done so.

Miles agreed to look into the circumstances under which the blood test had been taken and processed, to explore any possible irregularity that may have occurred. However, he did warn Peter that this was likely to be fruitless as the police were always careful to follow an exact procedure, particularly in serious circumstances such as these.

What would be hard to discount or challenge were the witness statements of the drivers he had overtaken at high speed. All had agreed he was travelling well above the statutory speed limit of forty miles per hour when the collision occurred.

So, it was agreed that morning that Miles would represent him, but that he could probably only have a small effect on the final sentence. He did point out that his presence would at least give Peter some moral support at a very harrowing time.

Peter lived alone, having been divorced several years earlier. At the large electronics company, where he worked, he held a senior board position. His hobbies were his motorbikes, he had three, and his acting in a local dramatic society.

It was at a rehearsal evening later in the week, when talking to a friend in the same society, that a possible escape from his predicament was proposed.

His friend, Julian, had found a website that advertised the arranging of escapes for people who were facing serious trouble ahead. Peter made contact with the website and was given travel instructions and the costs involved.

After a day or so of pondering the alternatives, he decided he would go, although he was most unsure of what the final outcome could be. He just knew he had to do something. Spending many years in prison was something completely unthinkable for him.

He called his solicitor and informed him of his decision to leave the UK. He didn't, however, disclose any further details as the website had made it crystal clear that in order for his escape to be successful, absolute secrecy was essential.

Peter was predictably scared. *If only I could turn the clock back*, he thought,

Chapter 4

Antonio Alcosta and his wife, Kokee, lived in Guatemala; it was they who set up this website called 'Pathways'. A website that would be attractive for people desperate to hide somewhere.

Antonio knew that a high fee could be charged for making their journeys to a new life and this alone would be a good benefit to them, but that was not their main reason for recruiting these people. These recruits would be expected to work their passage. A daring mission for them to undertake would await them all.

Antonio initially calculated that they would need eight well-performing recruits. However, allowance was made for the fact that all might not make the final journey nor would everyone eventually be up to the task being planned for them. For these reasons, they had set their sights and made plans on initially recruiting at least twelve people.

It was this website that had got Peter where he was now, sitting onboard this Boeing 777–300, getting ready for its non-stop flight to San Francisco.

A flight scheduled as such, but one that was not going to turn out that way!

Little did over two hundred passengers fastened into their seats know what was going to befall them in the coming hours.

Jayne Wilson was sitting near the front of the second class section in row 10. She was with her partner of fifteen years, Alan Crawford. At forty-seven years of age, he was five years her senior. They had lived in a well-furnished, comfortable, semi-detached three-bedroomed house on the outskirts of Woking. This was a small commuter town with a good train service to both London and the bank in Guildford, where they had both been employed. Alan had been the assistant manager at the branch prior to a raft of redundancies that had swept through the group. These had cost him his job just a year before.

He was bitter to be dealt this card, after over ten years of loyal service at the same branch, particularly as he had been unable to secure a similar position elsewhere since. Jayne was a teller on the customer-facing side of the branch. Alan had put her forward for the position.

They hatched the bank robbery together. He not only had a motive but also an intimate knowledge of the workings of the master safe security system.

He told Jayne that after a Monday morning cash delivery, there would be a great deal in the master safe. Based on this knowledge and a website they had found, they put their plan into action.

Jayne pretended to be pregnant and, after gradually padding out her clothing over a seven-month period, she now really looked the part. A friend agreed to advance order a £10,000 withdrawal from his business account, set for a Monday afternoon at the start of July.

This was a popular time with many people wanting cash for their holidays, so the safe would certainly be very well-stocked! A withdrawal of this size required the large master safe to be opened with advanced warning. Their friend entered the branch and approached Jayne's till. He made the prearranged withdrawal request. She set the timed safe to open ten minutes later. He sat and patiently waited.

After ten minutes, she went to the safe in the back room. She took out the cash for the customer but also emptied the entire contents of the huge safe and put it on the floor beside it. She then went back to her customer and completed the transaction.

A few minutes later, she went back for her fifteen-minute routine break.

She emptied a large amount of stuffing from her clothing and replaced it with all the money in custom-made pockets, ones that had been carefully made.

She then told her manager she was suffering abdominal pains and asked to be allowed to go to see her doctor with some urgency. He immediately agreed, of course.

She phoned her partner, Alan, and he quickly drove to the bank to collect her. He was, of course, expecting the call. She slowly and purposefully walked out of the branch. Little did any of the staff know that this was the last time they would see her! The pair went to a quiet car parking area previously planned on. She took all of the money out of the pouches on her person and tucked them carefully away in their pre-packed cases.

They then went directly to the long-term car park at Heathrow and, along with their pre-packed cases, they proceeded to the departure terminal. So far, all was going to their plan. They then joined a short queue to get through the check-in process. At the departure gate, they felt a mixture of excitement and apprehension as they waited for the call to board.

Both were relieved to have got this far, but still very concerned as to the final end to this daring mission.

Finally, they successfully got on board and were settled in their seats together. The pair looked at each other, held hands, and couldn't hide their excitement at the pending takeoff. They had done it.

They had got together as an item after meeting at a nightclub in Windsor called The Rik a Tik. Somewhere that became famous for being the launching pad for pop artists such as Alan Price and Georgie Fame! They danced together a couple of times and that was it. They simply clicked!

They were very happy together. Both shared a joint interest in music, good food, and films; Alan was a walking encyclopaedia of movies. He knew just about everything about any film you could mention. Who acted in it, who directed and produced it, as well as knowing the entire plot, of course! They watched at least two new films a week on their subscribed channels. To get the best of them, their TV was seventy-five inches, smart, and the sound was a 5.1 surround system around their comfortable lounge.

They didn't mind leaving this furnished rented property behind but, although this system was theirs, they obviously couldn't take it with them. So, it was something they would eventually have to replace.

George Middleton was born in 1954. It was the year that the Great Britain national rugby league team beat France to win the first Rugby League World Cup at the Parc des Princes in Paris. That was quite a coincidence, as later at school, he was very keen on playing in the top team in the county. It was also the year that Roger Bannister became the first person to break the four-minute mile, at the road track at the University of Oxford's campus.

To complete his birth year's major events, Christmas day saw the tragic Prestwick air disaster. A BOAC Boeing 377 Stratocruiser crashed on landing at Prestwick Airport in poor visibility, taking twenty-eight lives.

His birthplace was Liverpool but, at just four years of age, his parents relocated to Chester. They chose to start him at what they saw as a better school than those that were available in Liverpool. His parents gave him the best education they could afford, but he never excelled at any particular subject. He left school at sixteen with just a few, low-grade GCSE qualifications. He had no career plan at that time, but later made good friends of a skilled plumber who taught him the trade.

He eventually set up his own independent business and made a reasonable living.

He was always ready to work on a Sunday to deal with emergencies for which, he had learnt from his friend that, substantial rates for this special service could be charged.

He often told people of one incidence when he and his friend attended one of these Sunday emergencies. They fixed the problem in thirty minutes, for which they submitted an invoice for £20. A great deal in those days. When the property owner protested saying, "I am a London stockbroker and I don't earn that much!"

His friend replied, "Neither did I when I was a stockbroker!" They got paid and laughed all the way to the pub.

George managed to remain single, mainly due to working extremely long hours and socialising very little, until he was thirty-eight. In the years that followed, his marriage to Maria was satisfactory, but it was never passionate nor deep. After about thirty years together, he wasn't sure of exactly how many as they never bothered to celebrate, his life had become mundane and without any excitement.

He had retired at sixty-six years of age and was bored with life in general. He often wondered that perhaps it would have been different, more fulfilled, if they had raised children.

Then, suddenly, excitement appeared in the most unexpected way! He became a winner of the UK lottery! When George first realised he was one of the winners of this weekly lottery, he was of course shocked. He just couldn't believe it. He checked over and over, but there was no doubt he was going to take at least a generous share of the jackpot. He said nothing to his wife. Being a rather old-fashioned couple, they had always held separate bank accounts. For what was about to happen, this was most fortunate for George.

The money was finally credited to his account about ten days later. He just kept looking at his balance online in amazement, and some shock, but also excitement. It was just over £6 million. He had ticked the 'no publicity' box on the necessary paperwork and had told not a living soul.

Nobody that was except his bank manager, who was also able to put him in touch with a company offering a service to help him keep this money away from his wife! He contacted the same website that the others had done.

They helped him transfer the lottery winnings to a numbered, secure, off shore bank account prior to boarding this plane, getting ready to depart the UK for San Francisco.

As he sat there, he wondered what his wife, Maria, would make of the note he had left beside her bed. He had told her he was leaving but made no mention of where he was going, or why. He moved his seat back a little from its upright position, closed his eyes, and tried to relax.

Chapter 5

Angela McHaig was another with a past to hide. She had been a semi-professional singer from Dundee, Scotland. Her singing career started by being a very active member of the local church choir. Her voice was so good that she was usually the one chosen to sing solos at evensong. Later, she formed a small group with two friends, one of which was her live-in partner and girlfriend. They toured around Scotland's pubs and clubs and became quite well-known locally. They made several fruitless attempts to get a recording contract from different record labels but were repeatedly disappointed to be turned down.

Following a traumatic and very emotional breakup with her partner, who moved out early one morning whilst she was asleep, the group was disbanded and she finally went solo. She quickly secured a performing contract to sing nightly at a chain of clubs in the area.

Now, at thirty-eight years of age, she had become tired of the same performances over and over again. She felt it was high time to retire. She had earned a good deal of money during her career and lived a very comfortable lifestyle in a lovely four-bedroomed detached house in a quiet suburb of the city. She had put it up for sale a few weeks before and had achieved a quick £700,000 sale. She then rented a small apartment to enjoy her early retirement. Angela celebrated with one last performance at a local club. Afterwards, she held a private party for a small group of friends.

Inevitably, during the course of the evening, she drank a great deal, due to her high spirits. Because her new apartment so was close by, she decided to risk driving home. Something she should never have done and something she came to bitterly regret.

She just didn't see the young man using the zebra crossing and hit him with considerable force. He was thrown to the pavement and badly injured. Angela promptly panicked and drove even faster to flee the scene as quickly as possible. She put her car into the small garage which was included with the apartment rental, went inside, and locked the front door. Her heart was pounding. Would he be ok? Had anyone seen her car? She went to bed and somehow managed to go into a deep sleep.

She was abruptly awakened by knocking on her front door at 7.45 am. Her worst fears were realised. The accident had been caught on CCTV by a nearby office camera and her number plate had been recorded. After examining her car to view the damage, the police cautioned her, made the arrest, and drove her to the local police station. Here, she was given a blood test and questioned at length as to the events that had transpired. She was charged with several offences including leaving the scene of a serious accident.

She made a full statement and was held in custody until the following morning. At 10 am, she found herself before a judge in the nearby law courts, where a short statement was read out. She pleaded guilty and a date was set for a trial the following month. She was then released on bail.

The following day, she checked with the local hospital as to the injuries of the young man. This only made her more depressed and concerned for her future; he was on life support and in a coma with suspected brain damage. His back was also broken in two places. She left the hospital in tears.

Shortly, she contacted a website trading under the name of 'Pathways'. This was the same one some others on this flight had also used. Now, she was sitting in this same plane awaiting final departure checks before takeoff.

Sitting in seat 4A, first class, was Abdul Singh. He was a wealthy Indian man who had made a small fortune from trafficking drugs; cocaine mainly. Although he now lived in Southall, South London, with his wife, Natasha, and his thirteen-year-old son, Ruben, he was born and brought up in Bangalore (also known as Bengaluru). This town was the centre of India's high-tech industry and he spent his early years working for a major camera lens manufacturer. He was brought up to speak the local language, Kannada, but his work necessitated a good command of the English language. This proved to be no problem for Abdul.

Their son was named Ruben after his own late father. At seven years of age, his son was not doing well at their local school. Abdul could see that their education system was well below the standard he wanted for him. He, therefore, decided their family should leave Bangalore and relocate to the UK. From his business dealings, he could see the education there was far superior to anything he could achieve in Bangalore. The catch was the cost involved. His wages in the camera lens company would never be enough so he started looking for other earning possibilities.

Whilst he didn't agree with drug taking, and certainly didn't want his son to be involved, he could see that drugs could be a lucrative business. He spent some time researching and soon managed to establish some useful contacts in this trade. Prior to moving to the UK with his wife and son, he used these to set up his own UK dealing business.

He thought he was bulletproof in these dealings, but one night, a knock on his door by two Scotland Yard detectives told a different story. He had been tracked down by an undercover officer and a search warrant was issued to enter his home and search it. They quickly found a sizeable stash of class-A drugs and over twenty thousand in used notes. A list of contacts was also uncovered that would surely lead to further arrests. He was charged at a local police station and released on bail; pending his upcoming trial. That was a court appearance he had no intention of attending. He too had made it to this plane with his wife and son, all set to leave the UK for the safety of a new home elsewhere, again, thanks to 'Pathways'.

Abdul, his wife, and son now totalled twelve passengers all aboard, comfortably seated and awaiting their flight to take them away for their fresh start. But there was one more person on board who was a vital part of this plan to make the total of thirteen escapees. The remaining one was on the flight deck; he made up the complete list of those attempting to escape their previous lives.

The remaining normal fare-paying passengers onboard totalled a further two hundred and twenty-two souls.

On the flight deck were two pilots. The captain was James Robert Buckland; who had been a British Airways pilot for twenty-one years and had been promoted to his captain status just three years earlier. He was sitting in the left-hand seat, as was the custom of all airlines. On his right was Matt Dunbar, his co-pilot. He had been with BA for just fifteen months, having previously flown with Ryanair for six years beforehand.

James, Jamie to his small circle of friends, lived in Sandhurst, close to the military academy school there. This was an exclusive, expensive housing area. It was, however, something his six-figure salary could comfortably afford. He was married and had four children. One of them would have had a twin brother had he not passed away at birth. It was a harrowing time for the family. His eldest was at a boarding school in Oxford, where he was excelling in science and maths subjects. He wanted to follow in his father's footsteps and become a pilot too. James loved his job, although he was once overheard describing these long-haul flights as 'hours of boredom, in dispersed with moments of blind panic!'.

Having said that, his wife always told their friends that she had no worries for his safety when flying. She was just relieved to hear he had safely navigated his Jaguar car to his parking spot at the airport. She firmly believed that aircraft were far safer than cars. Statistically, she was, of course, quite correct.

Matt had a particularly disturbing history. Right from the tender age of just eleven, his father could see he was different from other boys of his age. He was physically attracted to very young girls, mostly much younger than himself. His mother noticed nothing amiss. As he matured into puberty and beyond into his mid-teens, he still tended to spend time anywhere he could be with very young girls. He even started a youth club to spend time with them. Several complaints from parents eventually ensued and, whilst no action was ever taken, he quietly closed the weekly club.

In truth, he had physically molested several very young girls and was accused of exposing himself on one occasion. He was always careful, however, to ensure that on any occasion when these things occurred, there were no witnesses.

It was, therefore, one word against another. One being a child in each case. It was several years later that his big mistake was made.

Online, he slowly groomed a thirteen-year-old girl from Oldham. She was only a schoolchild, of course. They exchanged emails, often enclosing explicit photos. Matt naturally had sent much younger pictures of himself, none showing his real age of thirty-four. He presented himself as a very fit-looking twenty-one-year-old. He sent semi-naked male pictures to her that weren't his. He encouraged her to send naked pictures of herself to him. She did so. There were emails discussing her puberty and period commencement. All this came out later. He arranged to meet her at a local beauty spot; somewhere quiet and discrete.

Before the 'date', Julia's mother spotted an email interchange on her daughter's bedroom computer. She was shocked at what she read. She challenged her tearful daughter about what had been going on. She promptly alerted the local police, who responded immediately. They set up a 'sting' to have an officer meet Matt at the prearranged spot and time. He was there and, despite repeated denials, was cautioned and arrested.

Matt spent twenty-four hours in custody undergoing intense questioning. The email evidence recovered from his computer alone was more than enough to charge him. He appeared in court the following day for an initial hearing. The charge was read out and he pleaded guilty.

After fixing a future date for a trial, his lawyer managed to achieve a release on bail. He left the court with no intention of returning.

His lawyer put him in touch with a website, telling him that they could not only solve his problem but theirs too; as will become evident shortly…

Matt didn't actually meet anyone, they remained anonymous, just as they had with all of the others. What was different though is that he received written instructions as to his role in the escape for them all. It covered every detail. He was then the only escapee who knew the whole plan, including what would hopefully be their final destination!

On the flight deck, both pilots were busy going through their final departure checks. Because this was so routine and rarely found any discrepancies, missing something through a lack of concentration was easily possible. Because of this, being a very experienced pilot, James usually went through this procedure more carefully than many younger pilots. He often checked even the most basic things several times. It was most surprising, therefore, that neither he nor his co-pilot noticed the lower-than-normal oil pressure on engine number two. It was something they would both later regret.

Chapter 6

A middle-aged man, who introduced himself as David, was in the aisle seat of row 15, opposite Peter Andrews. The middle seat between them was empty giving extra comfort to them both. David struck up a conversation with Peter about how busy the airport was and how slow all the security checks had been. Peter was actually focused on his mission, just to get away, but tried to seem interested and friendly to this stranger. They discussed San Francisco and particularly 'Silicon Valley' where David was heading. It turned out that he worked for one of the large semiconductor manufacturers as their UK sales manager.

He told Peter that this was his ninth visit to the 'Valley' during the past thirteen years of working for them. His company was a spin-off from a much larger one, headed up by a very bright engineer who had developed a new technology for image transmission by a very clever compression method. It reduced the memory required, the transmission time and hence the cost. His company was doing well and he explained that he was hopeful that his stock options would eventually give him a comfortable retirement.

Peter tried to show interest in all of this but his mind was elsewhere. He, of course, had remorse for the dreadful accident he had caused and the horrific result that ensued, but his first thoughts were for himself and his future. He must have expressed his interest in David's stories because he just didn't stop. Tale after tale almost put Peter to sleep!

On the flight deck, the pilots completed all the required checks and confirmed to air traffic control that they were ready for pushback. A few minutes later, they were given this clearance. They taxied towards runway 7L as instructed and awaited the final go-ahead for takeoff. They waited patiently for a lengthy period; rather longer than usual. This was due to the runways all being exceptionally busy with landing many inbound aircraft. At one point, the captain was becoming seriously concerned about the amount of fuel they were wasting.

The last thing he wanted was for their supply to drop below the safe level which would mean returning to the stand for a top-up. He needn't have worried as the go-ahead to take off at will was given in the nick of time.

The engines were powered up and the huge plane began accelerating down the runway. Whilst many passengers, not altogether comfortable with flying, tensed in their seats, clenching white knuckles, there were a dozen who heaved a deep sigh of relief. They were finally getting away from the UK and the danger it would have had in store for them, had they remained. It was hard to say who was the most relieved; all had serious problems that they were running away from.

They were almost at takeoff speed, known as 'V1' when the instruction "rotate" would be given to lift off, when a loud bang came from the left-hand side engine. Immediately, almost by instinct, the captain shouted, "Abort, abort!" The engines were shut down and airbrakes were applied, along with foot brakes. Finally, engine number one was put into reverse to further slow the plane's rapid approach towards the end of the runway. The plane stopped safely in good time, due to the quick responses of the pilots.

This had been one of those moments of 'blind panic' that the captain had described. He pondered for a moment at what his wife would be feeling if she had known about this emergency. The co-pilot reported the issue to the control tower and received the instruction to move slowly off the runway onto an emergency exit on the left side. The captain, realising that the passengers must have been disturbed by this experience, quickly made an announcement.

"Ladies and gentlemen, this is your captain speaking. I am sorry that it was necessary to abort our takeoff at the last moment, but a fault developed in one of the engines, as those of you sitting on the left-hand side of the plane will surely have noticed. We will await a fire tender, which will come out as a precaution. Then, we will probably be instructed to de-plane you all here and you will return to the terminal building by coach. We will then make other arrangements for your flight today. Thank you in advance for your patience, and again, we apologise for this unavoidable delay."

The passengers were of course agitated at this experience but some were more concerned than others, some were more anxious to get away than others. Peter Andrews was now feeling sick with worry. It was not only the prospect of going back to the terminal, but also he knew there was now the real possibility of an overnight stay in an airport hotel. His past experiences told him that finding another plane and crew would take time.

Jayne Wilson and her partner, Alan Crawford, were sweating in panic. They both knew that within a very short while after leaving her bank with the contents of the safe, the theft would have been discovered and the alarm raised. The police were surely already looking for them. The prospect of remaining in the UK overnight was indeed a daunting one for them.

Unknown to Abdul Singh, the police had already discovered he, his wife, and his son had made a run from his drug trafficking trial and were in the process of checking all the obvious escape routes, including of course all UK airports. Every one of the thirteen escapees had their own anxieties at this unforeseen setback. One that could prove to be a disaster for any of them. It was a situation none of them had anticipated or wanted.

Eventually, after what seemed an age, two fire tenders came alongside the plane and engineers in another vehicle got out. They then began inspecting the faulty engine. It was clear that there was considerable visible damage to it.

Later it was discovered that there had been an oil leak from the engine concerned. This leak was minor to begin with, only showing a slightly lower-than-normal pressure reading on the flight deck and not enough to trigger the warning lights. However, during taxiing to the runway, the leak increased and once the engines were fired up to full power, the leak vastly increased due to the engine's speed of rotation. Subsequently, an internal explosion occurred, causing the engine to cease any output power at all.

After a few minutes, the flight crew were instructed to open the doors and deploy the emergency escape slides. All passengers were instructed to remove their shoes and glasses, leave all personal belongings behind, and take turns exiting the plane in this rather ungainly manner. Of course, most ignored the 'leave all belongings behind' instruction and held on tightly to their valuables, leaving them securely on their person! One by one, on each of the two right-hand slides, passengers exited the ill-fated plane.

For safety, doors and slides on the left side of the plane, where the faulty engine was, were not used. They all were instructed to keep together in an orderly group to await transport back to the terminal building. Slowly, a stream of several coaches ferried the passengers to the safety of the terminal. Soon, all were back where they had started not long before. On entering the building, security staff took all passports from the passengers for further checks. This was particularly concerning for some.

Natasha turned to her husband, Abdul, and quietly quizzed, "Why are they taking our passports away from us?"

"I have no idea," he said. "It is most irregular but we must hope it does not indicate there could be a problem for us." Others were also questioning this action and were becoming increasingly agitated. What they hadn't considered, however, was that their luggage had to be removed and married up with each passenger correctly. Eventually, a senior member of the ground security staff made an announcement.

"Ladies and gentlemen, as you are aware a fault developed on your aircraft, one serious enough to justify aborting the takeoff at the last moment. The plane is being examined as we speak and we expect a verdict as to its airworthiness shortly. In the meantime, we are now taking you to a holding lounge where you will be offered complimentary refreshments. We expect to be able to update you with more information very shortly."

All the passengers were then directed along a long corridor to this holding lounge. It was comfortable with plenty of seating for everyone. Copies of a drinks and snacks menu were circulated around the small tables. All were listed as complimentary, except alcoholic beverages, which had sky-high prices listed beside each one. Many passengers felt the need to order alcoholic drinks to calm their shaken nerves. Almost all grumbled at having to pay for them and the somewhat excessive prices being charged.

Most had the means to pay, having kept hold of either cash or credit cards.

After they had left the plane, there was much talk around this lounge. Some speculated as to the cause of the aborted takeoff, but most were simply interested in when exactly they would be getting away. Some thought it would not be before long, but the more experienced travellers, such as Peter Andrews, were inclined to believe they would not be flying again that day. More than an hour passed, slowly, with no news.

Alan Crawford was feeling particularly agitated, knowing the bank would have surely alerted the police many hours ago and they would therefore be the subject of a 'manhunt'. He strode up to the airline information desk and aggressively demanded an update on a rescheduled flight time. He shouted for all to hear, "How much longer are you going to hold us here with no information?" Many probably thought him rude and aggressive, but nevertheless listened intently for any reply that could throw further light on this painful delay.

The gentleman on the desk informed him that they were still awaiting news of the technical issue and assured him that they would all be updated shortly.

He also promised to chase up the airline for any possible news that he would then be able to impart. Almost immediately, he was seen quietly speaking to someone on the telephone but he couldn't be heard. His wife, Jayne, chastised him for unnecessarily drawing attention to them, both knowing that a low profile would probably have been a better option! However, nobody thought badly of his actions. Some could almost have clapped him for his courage!

Chapter 7

Angela sat in a corner, alone. She didn't speak to anyone. Some noticed the large quantities of alcohol she seemed to be drinking. Those closest to her would probably have counted three large vodka and tonics during the previous hour. She was clearly trying to calm her nerves. Drinking quite heavily was actually routine for her. She had recognised her drinking problem some years before and had briefly attended Alcoholics Anonymous. Attendance to these meetings didn't last long. After only a handful of sessions, she quit. Attending the sessions that is, not her drinking! She soon returned to her habit.

Angela was, of course, concerned for the condition of the young man she had so seriously injured but, what was most prominent in her mind was what would be her fate. As a rather selfish, self-centred person, she had always put herself first in every situation.

George Middleton was sitting alone in another corner, drinking his second coffee. He wondered what his wife would be doing or thinking. He knew that the police do not go looking for someone who has just run away, leaving a note. He would not be classed as a missing person, justifying police time. Time that could be better spent on other matters.

He also had assumed that his wife would have no idea about his lottery win and therefore his reason for leaving. At sixty-eight years of age, she would surely think it unlikely he would have run off with another woman, especially as there had been no previous indication of any other relationship. He tried to put these thoughts out of his mind and instead, to think positively of things he was going to do with the money! It was a sum too large for him to fully digest.

Almost another hour passed before a member of airport ground staff came in and made a further announcement.

"Ladies and gentlemen, we are able to confirm that the aircraft you were on has a serious engine problem which makes it impossible to be put back into service today. We had been trying to find an alternative one for you, but have been unsuccessful unfortunately." Sighs could be heard all around.

He went on to say, "We will be taking you all to nearby hotels by coach. As there are so many of you, you will be shared around several different ones. Families will, of course, not be split up."

He then explained that the stay and meal vouchers would be covered by the airline. Finally, he confirmed that the airline expected to add an additional flight for them all together the following afternoon, with an exact time to be confirmed in the morning. He informed them that their luggage was already en route to the appropriate hotels. All were at least glad to get some positive news, even if it meant a further delay to their San Francisco flight.

Most were grateful that the engine fault had developed before takeoff and not after!

Matt, the co-pilot, was particularly concerned as he knew he was a vital part of the escape for the thirteen of them. How would he be able to join them on the new flight now? It was imperative that he did! The other twelve had no idea what the plan was and how vital Matt was, so this was of no immediate concern to them.

Matt needn't have worried. Within minutes, he and the captain were taken to an interview room and were required to give a full debrief as to the engine failure and the aborted landing. Following this, a senior member of the airline entered the room. He said, "We realise you may have had other plans, but we would like you to remain in this hotel if possible and pilot the replacement aircraft tomorrow."

The captain had no plans for the following day, other than being in San Francisco. It was only the day after that concerned him as it was to have been a day off with his wife to celebrate her birthday. He told him that she put great store on birthdays and always planned these weeks in advance. Jamie knew that to let her down would cause great disappointment for her, their children, and all the friends who had been invited to share the day. He, therefore, declined the offer and politely, but firmly, asked to be allowed to return home.

This request was immediately granted. Matt was more than keen to stay with this passenger list and accepted in the knowledge that he would have another captain to 'deal with'. In reality, he didn't mind who it would be as long as the carefully planned procedure could be executed. He also had thought this captain was rather snobbish and he had taken a dislike to him immediately. He hadn't been looking forward to being in such enclosed proximity to him for many hours.

So, off to their respective hotels, they all went for a chill out before the following day. On arrival at their allocated hotels, all of the passengers found their luggage in reception and on check-in, found that the hotel staff were holding their passports as a check of both them and their respective luggage.

After being given keys to their rooms, the hotel porters transported their luggage for them. For some, this stay was a welcome relaxation, for others, it was going to be a particularly stressful and long night ahead.

The Holiday Inn Hotel's restaurant was packed to capacity with people waiting to get their turn for a dinner table. Thanks to the influx of passengers from the ill-fated San Francisco flight, the hotel was now fully booked with hungry guests. Following the Covid pandemic, this was a first for this hotel for many months.

Peter Andrews had found a table which, due to overbooking, he was forced to share with two others. They were a German couple heading home to Munich after their all too short holiday in the UK. Their very early morning flight made an overnight stay the most convenient for them. They introduced themselves, in perfect English, as Helmut and Olga. Peter was trying to relax and was quite happy for a distractive chat with these friendly people.

Helmut asked, "Are you awaiting a flight tomorrow too?"

Peter replied, "Yes, to San Francisco; today's was cancelled due to a technical problem with our plane." He went on to explain the dramatic events that had occurred with the aborted takeoff.

Helmut's wife, Olga, said, "That must have been frightening for everyone."

Peter replied, "Perhaps for some who were not seasoned flyers such as myself. I have had this kind of experience before." He then told a similar story about an aborted takeoff in Helsinki, Finland, three years before.

He went on, "We were going down the runway with full power when the takeoff was aborted at the last second. We were on an ice-covered runway, something quite normal in Finland." He explained and continued, "The captain came on the intercom and announced that the engines were not fully warmed up and the output power was too low. He told us he would go again. Sure enough he did and we took off perfectly. However, I know he lied to us because it is a fact that a jet engine achieves full power when cold with no problem. The truth was that he had not quite built up enough speed on the ice. The second time, he had the engines on full power before releasing the brakes. We then took off down the runway like a bullet!"

The German couple went on to tell Peter how much they had enjoyed their first holiday in the UK; they had hired a car and travelled extensively in just a one-week stay. They told him that they had been particularly looking forward to visiting Coventry as it had been a famous place in history. They had read that Lady Godiva had ridden through the streets naked on horseback in a protest of some kind and wanted to find out more. They, however, admitted that they found out little and that Coventry had been a disappointment to them.

Peter told them that his uncle had been a bank manager in that town and, because a large tractor manufacturer called Massey Ferguson was situated there and was one of his major account holders, he was able to get him a guided tour of the plant. Whilst Peter was only nine at the time, he explained that he had a vivid memory of the day.

This leading farm equipment manufacturer, with the exception of the engines and tyres, made every single part of their tractors there. He recounted seeing a red-hot steel chassis being lowered into cooling oil to temper it. The flames and heat were memorable. This all made for a relaxing conversation for them both.

Abdul Singh and his family were lucky to get their own table quite quickly. It was to be luck that didn't follow them for long…They all placed their orders for dinner. Food they would never get to eat.

Unknown to this family, or indeed any of the guests in the restaurant, two police cars had pulled up outside, both parked on the yellow lines right outside reception. (Strange how the police do not seem to have to follow any of the laws us humble citizens have to, whether they are on an emergency or not!) Two burly male officers got out of one car and a female constable got out of the other. All three of them went to the hotel reception desk together. They enquired to see the passports of the Singh family. All three were presented by the hotel manager. They enquired as to what room(s) they were in. The manager told them but explained that he knew the family had just gone through to dinner in the main restaurant on the first floor.

In order not to risk a scene in the busy restaurant, the police decided to ask a senior member of staff to go there and ask the husband to come to reception to speak with someone who was asking for him. A few minutes later, Abdul appeared at reception. After reading him his rights, he was arrested, put swiftly into handcuffs, and taken to one of the waiting police cars. The remaining two officers went discretely into the restaurant and asked Natasha and her son to also accompany them to reception.

There, Natasha was given the same treatment, immediately handcuffed and taken to join her husband in the first police car.

Their son, Ruben, was taken into the nearby lounge with the female officer and the situation was tactfully explained to him. He was asked if he had someone, preferably a family member, that he could stay overnight with. Through tears, he managed to tell them his aunt lived nearby in Hayes and he was sure she would be happy to let him stay. He gave them the address and they left together in the second car.

Meanwhile, Abdul and his wife were taken to Southall police station and, after being allowed to have something to eat and drink, they were put behind bars overnight. For them, there was clearly going to be no flight to San Francisco the next day; indeed if ever. Meanwhile, all the other passengers settled in for the night in their respective hotels.

It was clear at this point that the faulty engine on their plane was going to cost BA a great deal in sundry costs alone.

Unknown to anyone, this was not the only delay they would all soon be suffering.

Wan Lung was born in a small town called Liaoyang, about fifty miles south of Shenyang, in Northern China. He was one of four children, all boys. His father died of asbestosis when Wan was just five years old. He had worked in a factory making asbestos sheets for the building industry. It was working and breathing in the constant dust that claimed his life at just thirty-two years of age. His mother brought them all up on very limited resources. He lived on little more than a diet of rice and beans. She passed away just two years before he had set out on this expedition.

He had moved to the UK ten years before and had seen a market for car entertainment systems which, whilst fetching high prices in the UK, were comparatively cheap if you knew the right contacts in China. He had all those he needed. Over a ten-year period, he had achieved massive sales, which resulted in a bank balance to date of well over £4 million. Despite spreading it around four different banks, the Inland Revenue were slowly finding it. No tax had been paid on this income, not a penny. That was why he was running. Most of this money had been transferred to an offshore numbered account and he was ready to hide anywhere where he could enjoy it without interference.

He sat and wondered what he would buy first. High on his list was a Ferrari. He had always wanted one, but owning one in the UK would have drawn too much attention to himself and his wealth! The other thing toper most of his mind was to wonder where he, and the others on this journey, were going as their final destination. Would there be a Ferrari dealership there? Would there be roads suitable for that kind of car to stretch its legs? So many unknowns, slightly concerning, but at the same time quite exciting.

He went through to the hotel's restaurant and ordered a tuna salad and a bottle of champagne. The restaurant was full, mainly due to the passengers from the fated San Francisco flight, but of course, others were there too. He recognised a few faces from the flight and wondered what all their stories were. He knew he would have to wait until they all ended up together in their final destination; wherever that was going to be.

In the corner of the restaurant were the bank robbers, Jayne and Alan Crawford. They had deliberately chosen a secluded corner table that was conveniently placed next to an emergency exit. One they could use if needed. They had several worries. They knew the police must be on the lookout for them, probably checking ports of all kinds, however, they had managed to get through customs and immigration to get onto the plane earlier.

But then, that was very soon after the robbery. Much time had now elapsed and they surely would have to again face this procedure. The second issue was that both their cases had a large quantity of cash in them. They hadn't had any chance to count it, but expected it to total at least a million pounds! Would customs pick their contents up? They tried to relax but their eyes were everywhere, looking for possible trouble.

They had their meal but never really enjoyed it, nor probably even remembered what they had eaten. Eventually, the remaining ten of this 'escape party' retired to their rooms for the night. Few would probably sleep much. They didn't know when their new flight would be available, what time it would be or if they would get away at all. Little did they know, the police had already arrested one family and could be on the lookout for others.

Chapter 8

George Middleton had a particularly restless night and arose early. On going to his bathroom, he noticed a note that had been pushed under his door. It read: *There will be a meeting in the Great Banquet Hall at 11.30 this morning. Please attend, packed and ready to leave for the airport.* He, like all the others, realised that this was encouraging as it clearly indicated that a replacement flight had been secured. Hopefully, the last step of getting to San Francisco!

One by one, all others in the four hotels from the cancelled San Francisco flight read similar notes. All of them packed and went to their appropriate meeting venues in good time. Here, they were informed that they were all re-booked on a new BA flight departing at 4.20 that afternoon. They were told to be outside the front of their hotels at 1 pm ready to board their buses to take them to the airport terminal. They were further informed that their passports would then be returned to them, along with boarding passes and gate information.

Matt Dunbar, the co-pilot, didn't receive the same note that the fare-paying passengers had received. Instead, he had a visit from a BA official who gave him the flight information and informed him that a car would be outside his hotel at 12 noon. He was relieved to know he was set to fly a new aircraft that afternoon.

Matt was born in Ilford, Essex, in 1987, so was just thirty-six years old now. He was the only child of John and Maria. His father was a motor mechanic, working at a local garage in partnership with the owner. Maria was a registered childminder and looked after children of all ages at their home. It was when Matt was as young as just eight that he started exhibiting an interest in young girls. Of course, they were often in his house, being looked after by his mother. When Matt was about eleven and entering puberty, his father started to notice that his son had, what he saw as, undesirable sexual tendencies and expressed this concern to his wife.

She, however, reassured him that she could see nothing amiss but promised that she would keep a close eye on him whilst he was working the long hours he had to.

Just how many very young children he molested whilst living at home wasn't known. There were no complaints from any parents, so his mother was content that he was just a normal young lad. He left home at seventeen and rented a small flat nearby. To pay for this, he worked in a chocolate factory in the town. He started at the bottom, working on one of the fast-moving production lines.

The work was boring but a means to an end for him. He kept his head down and worked efficiently. After only two months, he was promoted to supervisor on good pay. That, along with a great deal of overtime, enabled him to obtain a pilot's licence.

It was then that he applied to Ryanair to become one of their pilots. His first application was turned down, mainly due to the time of year. It was winter and not their busiest time. In any event, there were always more applications than there were available positions. He didn't give up and applied again the following summer and this time, he was accepted. After going through extensive training with them, much at his own expense, he was certified to co-pilot their smaller planes. Six years went by and Matt did well with this airline. He kept a very timely schedule and seemed well-liked by his superiors.

He, eventually, trained and became qualified to fly their large wide-bodied planes, such as the 777. This gave him the opportunity to apply to BA to advance his career. So now, he was with BA and flying long-haul all over the world. This, of course, gave him many new opportunities to meet young girls. This had become some kind of utopia for him!

Joanna Crawley was in the Hilton, one of the better hotels local to the airport. She felt relaxed after a good night's sleep and sat down to a good healthy breakfast of fruit and nuts, washed down with a large glass of orange juice and a small black coffee. As a model, she had always looked after herself and kept in great shape. Her modelling career had gone well until she decided to take on extra night work at a lap dancing club. Her previous modelling had been for clothing with nothing more erotic than underwear.

However, this job required her to perform topless in a very brief thong. She always found it a little uncomfortable, but the pay was good and the tips were often very generous.

It was at this lap dancing club that she met a high-ranking member of the current government. All that transpired was supposed to be confidential. Shortly after a night spent in his hotel suite, a knock came on her door early one morning. She was read her rights, then arrested and taken to the local police station. It was here she found herself under suspicion of murder as the politician had been found dead soon after she had left his room. She was tracked down through the hotel CCTV system, which was installed throughout the hotel and crystal clear. After extensive and lengthy interrogation, she made a statement and was released on bail pending further investigation.

Jonathan Clarke was brought up in Southall, close to Heathrow Airport. He had enjoyed a moderately successful boxing career but had needed to take early retirement some twenty years before, at just thirty-three. He was previously doing well until he had come up against a far superior boxer, who gave him a devastating head blow that not only knocked him out instantly but gave him a blood clot on his brain.

An operation was considered risky and he was strongly advised to cease fighting. He didn't miss the money, he had enough, but he did miss the excitement and the adrenaline rush his fights generated. His record was excellent. He had only lost three fights out of the dozens he had fought.

He went, together with his son, Michael, to the breakfast room at their hotel. Here, they both enjoyed a most unhealthy, traditional English fry-up! Michael was a car mechanic at a small local garage where he had worked for the past nine years. He lived with his father in a comfortable house in Harlington, Middlesex, very close to the airport. His mother had died in a helicopter accident in the Grand Canyon some six years earlier, whilst on a holiday visiting her cousin in Phoenix, Arizona. There had been eight people onboard the helicopter that fateful Thursday afternoon. All were killed instantly.

Despite this, neither he nor his father seemed to have any misgivings about flying. They both realised that the chances of any flying accident were always extremely remote.

By 1 pm, all passengers were assembled outside their respective hotels with their luggage. One by one, buses came and ferried them back to the airport terminal. Bits of conversation took place between some of them whilst waiting in line at the check-in desks. Things such as 'Let's hope this plane has two engines' and 'Fingers crossed for this one' could be heard. The passengers needed to continue to be patient because neither of the two check-in desks allocated for this new flight were yet open. They had simply been brought to the terminal too early. It was 1.45 pm and the desks were not opening for another thirty minutes or so.

Eventually, at 2.30, both desks opened and the check-in staff began working their way through the lengthy line of passengers wanting to get aboard this replaced San Francisco flight. Once checked in, this huge London airport offered plenty for passengers to do 'airside' whilst waiting for up to two hours before boarding. Dozens of shops, restaurants, and bars. The shops were all claiming duty-free prices but were frequently selling goods at prices above even those found in the high streets! Novice travellers frequently fell prey to these shops. Seasoned travellers avoided them.

There were also bars with extortionate prices. All these businesses knew they had a captive market at this location!

A disturbance took place in an Irish bar called Murphy's. It started with an argument between two young men, both Irish from their accents. One had a shaven head, the other a ponytail.

Tattoos were clearly visible on one of them. The shouting and arguing got worse and resulted in blows being struck. All those nearby backed away as fists were thrown. Quite quickly, three burly security guards, who were fortunately patrolling nearby, appeared on the scene and separated the two men. After a short scuffle, both were put into handcuffs and removed from the bar. The staff quickly cleaned up the broken glass and spilt drinks. All then returned to normal. It was all handled so promptly and efficiently that it made one wonder if this kind of trouble was a frequent occurrence!

The remaining drinkers in the bar went back to their tables and continued their respective conversations as though nothing had happened. One of them was heard to remark that it was just like being at home in a downtown Dublin bar!

Eventually, the call they had all been waiting for came to summon all these passengers to their San Francisco flight. "Will all passengers travelling on flight BA317 to San Francisco this afternoon, please go immediately to Gate A22 where your flight is now ready for boarding." This is the call that anyone waiting to fly looks forward to, sometimes for two hours or more! These passengers were no exception. All immediately made their way through the numerous walkways to the appropriate gate. There was ample seating for everyone at this final departure area. The BA official at the door announced, "We will be boarding in seat order today, so can we first have all passengers with seat numbers from 20 to 32 please."

After all of them had their boarding cards checked and entered the huge Boeing 777, the remaining passengers were called to do the same. After about thirty minutes, all were safely on board, when there was the usual chaos of everyone scrambling for space in the overhead luggage racks.

Once all were seated, the cabin staff closed the large doors and secured them with large airtight locks.

These doors look sturdy and heavy, yet even the slightest built stewardess seems to secure them as required.

Sitting to the left of Matt was the new flight captain, Alistair Fitzgerald. They chatted briefly about the morning's breaking news of a new scandal in the royal family. There had been others recently too. Alistair told Matt that when he lived in Windsor, close to the famous castle, he had once seen the queen at very close quarters. Matt thought this was just bragging to show his superiority over him.

After a few moments, the captain made his announcement. "Good afternoon, ladies and gentlemen, my name is Alistair Fitzgerald, I am your captain. Welcome aboard this Boeing 777 on this lovely warm afternoon here in London. Along with my co-pilot, Matt Dunbar, we will be flying you to San Francisco today. Our flying time will be ten hours and forty minutes. We shortly will be given clearance to push back and then taxi out to our runway for takeoff. In the meantime, ensure your seatbelts are fastened, your seats are in their upright position and all table trays closed and locked."

A few moments later, he received a message from the control tower that he certainly hadn't expected. He was informed that there was a problem with two of his passengers and that airport police were on their way to remove them from the plane. The captain acknowledged this message and discretely asked the leading flight attendant to open the front left-hand door again. Those sitting near the front were puzzled as to why this was happening, but their questioning looks were ignored by the cabin crew. The two people being hunted today were Alan Crawford and Jayne Wilson—the bank robbers!

Whilst unsettling for Matt, he wasn't altogether surprised as he knew there were others running away from their own crimes on this plane. He was just relieved to hear that it was a couple that were being sought! He still remained on course to escape.

They were seated in row 18, seats B and C. There was a look of horror on several faces as two airport police entered the front. Once they passed each other, they could be heard heaving sighs of relief. Not so for the two seated in row 18. They were both asked to retrieve their hand luggage and were then escorted off the plane. Unknown to them, a sniffer dog had found two suitcases that aroused the suspicion of the airport security. On inspection, their jaws dropped…many thousands of used notes, mainly of the larger denominations, were packed inside each one. It didn't take the police long to put two and two together and work out the guilty pair's identity. There was to be no flight to freedom for this pair.

They would eventually join Abdul and Natasha Singh in prison. There was much speculation around the plane as to what the reason was for this couple's arrest. Of course, a few guessed that they most likely were to have been part of their escape group.

Chapter 9

So now, including the co-pilot, there were just eight would-be escapees on this plane; all hopeful of getting away. Now the plane's forward door was again closed and secured. After the crew had completed the usual extensive flight checks, the captain confirmed to air traffic control that they were ready for takeoff. They didn't need to wait long as the go-ahead to taxi to the runway was given, along with clearance to take off at will. They eased the huge jet to the start of the runway and kept rolling as they throttled up accelerating to take off speed. "V1," the co-pilot called to signal to the captain to rotate and lift off the runway.

Everyone heaved a sigh of relief to be away at last, some twenty-eight hours later than originally planned. San Francisco was now firmly in their sights. Or so most thought…

Once the plane had reached its cruising height of thirty-six thousand feet, the course was set and the autopilot switched on. This now gave the pilots time to have a further chat and get to know each other. Alistair introduced himself to Matt.

He told him that he had recently moved house to live in Sonning, Berkshire. Matt knew this area as he had two friends living there. He knew it was a very exclusive suburb of Reading, which contained the famous Bluecoat boys' school, one that had been attended by royalty! This alone made it clear that this pilot was in a much higher salary bracket than he was. Little did this captain know what was to befall him long before the plane was eventually to reach San Francisco!

The cabin staff had plenty to do. A lot of preparation was needed to service over two hundred passengers with food and drinks throughout the next ten hours or so. They knew from years of experience that passengers fell into several clearly defined types. Between them, they were able to quickly categorise them, working out who would be demanding and hard work and who would be straightforward to take care of during this lengthy flight. It would be accurate to say that the seven escaping passengers were quiet and kept a low profile, so as not to draw unnecessary attention to themselves.

The passengers were about eight hours into their journey and had all enjoyed dinner; most had now settled down to get some sleep. At this point, it was about midnight British time, but for those who had already adjusted their watches to California time, it was just four in the afternoon!

The flight had approximately three hours left to run…or it would have, had it been going non-stop to San Francisco.

A couple of hours later, the pilots were chatting and it was then that Matt suggested they get some coffee to keep them alert. Alistair agreed that this was a good idea and two coffees were subsequently brought to the flight deck by Matt, who had taken the opportunity of a bathroom break at the same time. Unknown to Alistair, Matt had slipped a very strong sleeping sedative into the captain's coffee. It was just twenty minutes later that Alistair complained of feeling dizzy and said he was finding it hard to stay awake. Just ten minutes later, he slumped over his controls and was fast asleep. Matt immediately summoned the senior cabin attendant to the flight deck.

He told her, "I don't know what is wrong but he said he felt dizzy then just passed out. He seems to be breathing ok but I cannot rouse him." They agreed they couldn't move him back into the first-class cabin for fear of causing alarm to the passengers there, so they moved him into the 'jump seat' behind and fastened him securely in.

Matt told her he would need to divert the plane to the nearest airport, as it was not a safe procedure to fly with only one pilot. He said he would discuss it with local traffic control and keep her informed. He further told her to say nothing to anyone else until he knew more. She then went back to her duties.

Local traffic control informed him that the nearest landing strip he could use was at the Pinal Airpark in Marana, Tucson, Arizona. This was a fifteen hundred acre site where aircraft were retired, or mothballed when no longer required for service.

Several hundred planes were here in the desert. This location had been chosen for its all-year-round climate to protect these commercial planes from corrosion. Matt contacted the airport manager; his name was Jim Petty. He was experienced, having been manager there for more than ten years, and he quickly began the necessary preparations for this wide-bodied plane's arrival.

The facility was formally known as the Marana Army Airfield when it was first established in 1942. It was used as a training area during World War Two. It is now owned by Pinal County, who lease out the 'parking' spaces! A further source of income for this airfield is the tourists visiting to view the planes there. These tours came in by bus daily.

Jim confirmed that the six thousand eight hundred and fifty feet runway was sufficient for this Boeing aircraft and he gave him the coordinates needed for landing. He informed him that he had clearance to land at will.

Matt thought carefully for a few minutes planning what he was about to say, then he made his announcement. "Ladies and gentlemen, this is your co-pilot speaking. Unfortunately, our captain has become poorly and is not in full control of his faculties. There is no cause for alarm as I am also an experienced pilot and will continue to fly the plane, as indeed I have been doing for several hours now. However, it is not airline policy to fly with just one pilot for obvious safety reasons, so we will be diverting to the nearest airport where we will either pick up another pilot to replace him or if he recovers after treatment, we will continue on the last part of our journey."

"Please fasten your seatbelts, put your seats in the upright position, and stow the tables in front of you. Also, please switch off all electronic devices in readiness for landing at Pinal Airport in just a few minutes." Sighs and groans could clearly be heard throughout the plane. Everyone was now getting tired of these continuing delays. Many began speculating and worrying as to how long this new delay would take.

Pinal Airfield 'housed' several hundred aircraft. They ranged from small single-propeller planes to old 747 Jumbo jets. Airlines and private owners alike rented these spaces whilst their planes were temporarily surplus to requirements.

Visitors came weekly for guided tours around the huge site to view all the planes and to hear the history of each. The talking point today was that a group of wealthy Arabs had made an offer to buy one of the retired Austrian Airlines 747s with the aim of turning it into a five-star restaurant in Dubai.

Whilst the offer was too small and rejected, the Arab consortia were confident that patience would eventually give them the plane they wanted. The price offered was a carefully guarded secret, but it was believed to be only a few thousand US dollars. The plane was seventeen years old and they knew two things. Firstly, the owners would never put this fuel-inefficient plane back into service, and secondly, there were currently more planes than buyers to service the flying public at this time. They were also well aware that getting this plane ready to fly to Dubai and obtaining the required airworthiness certification would be costly.

On the flight deck, Matt was carefully making all the necessary checks to ensure he would safely land this huge plane on his own. He programmed the airfield coordinates into the flight computer. He then brought the 777 around to line up with this desert runway. His preparations were perfect. The huge airliner touched down exactly at the right point on the runway and full brakes, along with reverse engines and full flaps, slowed the plane comfortably and smoothly to come to a stop, well before the end of the dusty runway. He slowly eased the giant plane towards the previously designated parking spot that the airfield manager had allocated for him, close by the small terminal building.

The passengers had mixed feelings. This was turning out to be quite a tortuous journey to San Francisco. Not as expected in any way! Many felt relieved to be on terra firma again, but many were getting clearly frustrated with the endless delays that beset this journey. Of course, some were getting ever agitated at their failure to fully escape! Little did they yet know that this was all part of the plan, details of which were very shortly to be revealed to them.

Matt again came onto the intercom. "As you can see, we have now landed at Pinal Airport. This is an interesting place for you to spend what will probably be a couple of hours. Here, in the desert, aircraft that are no longer required for their past service but could have value for others, as working aircraft or as spares are stored. There are hundreds of them here, along with a large aircraft museum. There are bus trips around this massive airfield daily for paying visitors to see it all. I have just been informed by Jim Petty, the airport manager, that there are a few seats available for the next tour."

"We have chosen at random a few lucky passengers who are now invited to take these few spare seats on the next tour, which is just about to depart. These are with the compliments of British Airways. So will the following passengers please exit the plane now, taking all personal possessions with them?"

He then read out the names of the seven escapees. They promptly exited the aircraft complete with their hand luggage, which was all these seven had, now that the 'bank robbers' were no longer part of the group. This made the new plan moving forward easier as no hold luggage was required to be removed for any of them. Once on the tarmac, they were joined by the eighth person on this new journey—Matt Dunbar, the co-pilot! They all were taken to a small adjoining runway, where awaiting them was a Gulfstream 4, a sixteen-seat, twin jet engine plane.

This plane had been leased for the day by Antonio. An expense covered by Pathways! All now realised that they were all running away together and that this was all part of the escape plan. It was clearly time now to get to know each other. They would after all now be living together, for a while at least.

Meanwhile, back on the 777, passengers were instructed by one of the cabin crew to collect all their personal belongings and calmly exit the aircraft. As soon as all had disembarked, they were taken to a large cafeteria where they were offered further complimentary refreshments. They were informed that a new flight crew would be on their way and that their plane would be ready to make its last short hop to San Francisco in about two hours.

The flight captain, Alistair Fitzgerald, had by now come to, albeit naturally feeling a little groggy after the sedative Matt had dosed him with. He left the plane walking slowly on his own. He met with Jim Petty in his office. It was becoming clear that he was rapidly recovering from whatever it had been that had incapacitated him. He talked with Jim for some time explaining that he felt ready to pilot the plane now the last leg of its journey. Jim said that he felt responsible for this plane now it had landed at 'his' airfield and that he would require a doctor to examine him and clear him as fit to fly before the plane could depart the airfield. Alistair readily agreed to this proposal and a local doctor was called.

He arrived quickly and performed the full examination that Jim had requested. He passed with flying colours, although he was unable to offer any explanation for what had caused the unexpected blackout that had occurred. He was ready now to pilot this plane and over two hundred passengers to San Francisco at last.

Jim went into the cafeteria looking for Matt, the first officer required to rejoin Alistair on the flight deck of this Boeing 777. To his surprise, he drew a complete blank. Despite a thorough search of all toilets and rooms, there was not a sight of him anywhere.

Jim conveyed this startling fact to Alistair with dismay. It was clear to both men that without a co-pilot on the flight deck, no departure would be possible. He did offer a viable suggestion. He knew that amongst the passengers were two other off-duty BA pilots travelling back to their base in San Francisco. He gave their names to Jim and requested that he ask them to come forward to talk with him.

After a short while, both appeared in Jim's office. A brief discussion quickly ascertained that one of them was only qualified and experienced at flying smaller 737 planes. The other, Mick Peterson, whilst not yet fully qualified to fly this particular plane, was an experienced captain who had flown several other wide-bodied ones for many years. In addition, he had used the 777 flight simulator a total of seven times for both takeoffs and also landings. Whilst not fully qualified as a captain of this particular plane, it was clear he was more than capable of taking a first officer role on this flight deck along with Alistair.

It was agreed that the two should board the plane and begin the lengthy flight departure procedures needed to get this plane airborne and over two hundred passengers to their needed destination. Should Matt not be found in the next hour, then they would proceed to take this plane to the skies.

In the airfield café, Jim made an announcement. One that was most welcome. "Will you all please now re-board your plane as we are now ready to depart for your final short flight to San Francisco." This was met with jubilation and eventually applause. He went on, "As we have no facility for printing boarding passes here, please just show your passports at the gate and proceed to the aircraft to sit in any seat you choose."

On board the Gulfstream, Matt Dunbar made a new announcement to his seven 'special' passengers.

"By now, you must all realise we are in this together, thanks to 'Pathways'. We will shortly take off for your final flight today. It will be to Guatemala City Airport. The flight will be about four hours. Please sit back and relax, you are almost 'home'."

There were just eight rows of seats with one on each side of the aisle. In seats 1A and 1B were Jonathan Clarke and his son, Michael. Behind them in 2A and 2B were Joanna Crawley and Angela McHaig. In the third row, seats 3A and 3B were occupied by Peter Andrews and George Middleton. Finally, in the fourth row, sitting alone in seat 4A was Wan Lung.

They all looked at each other, wondering what each had done to find themselves in this position. There was some conversation, but only sporadically, as all were not only tired but also each felt a little guarded about disclosing their past in any detail.

True to the earlier commitment made, two hours later, the remaining two hundred and twenty-two passengers were invited to return to their plane, which was now ready to depart the airfield with its fresh flight crew. They were told they could sit as they wished as printing boarding passes was not something this airport could do. Once on board, many were in different seats, none noticed that a few passengers were missing.

Meanwhile, back in London, interviews were taking place in two separate rooms at the same police station in Southall. Alan and Jayne were questioned by their lawyer, who eventually turned up, having made them wait eight hours. It was a simple cut-and-dried case to be prepared. The bank cameras had captured everything, the money had been found in their luggage, and a strip search by a female officer had revealed the fake pregnancy. They were held overnight, pending a court appearance the following day. At the subsequent hearing, they of course pleaded guilty as there was nothing different that they could have realistically done. At the trial that took place later that month, they were both handed jail terms.

Alan was given eight years as the mastermind behind the plan and Jayne received six years as a co-conspirator. These were considered lenient by some, but it was because neither had any previous convictions. Alan's emotional upset at having been treated harshly by the bank after years of loyal service was also taken into account by the judge. Both could expect parole at half these terms for good behaviour, should they choose.

In another interview room, a more serious case was being investigated. Abdul and Natasha had previously been captured and charged with a series of drug offences but had broken the bail terms and had run away from the previously arranged court hearing. They were both held in custody until a new trial date could be set. Their son continued to be taken care of by his aunt in Hayes.

It was not until six weeks later that the trial finally did take place. It was a fairly brief affair and little sympathy was shown by the judge. The defence's pleas for leniency seemed to fall on deaf ears. She stated that their trade in class-A drugs inflicted misery on addicts and their families. She gave them both the same sentence, the maximum she could, fourteen years behind bars; also, all drugs and monies found to be impounded, never to be returned.

On board the 777, all passengers were settled into their chosen seats, many in different ones from before. For this reason, nobody noticed that there were eight people missing. Once airborne, one stewardess commented to another that she had not seen the Chinese man who had previously requested an extra pillow. She remembered he had been in row 17. They also knew that the co-pilot, Matt, had gone missing, so they decided to do a new headcount. This, to their surprise, showed a difference of eight people from the original manifest. They were shocked but knew that other than informing the captain, nothing could now be done about it.

Chapter 10

Guatemala is bounded to the north and west by Mexico, to the northeast by Belize and (along a short coastline) by the Gulf of Honduras, to the southeast by El Salvador, and to the south by the Pacific Ocean. At the last census two years before, its total population had been recorded at around sixteen million. The main language of these inhabitants is Spanish.

Two years before hatching their plan, Antonio and his wife founded Pathways and began looking for the people they needed for a daring mission. The plan would take time and hard work by their recruits but they were determined to do whatever they had to in order to ensure its success.

It all began when a group of ruthless criminals moved into the area. They had a clear and evil plan. All four of them were very skilled card sharks and knew every trick there was to beat any system. They had honed their 'art' over several years and were a devastating force when working together. Two of them were brothers, born and raised in Campeche, a small town on the northwest coast of Mexico. They had set out on a life of crime from an early age.

They made friends with two similarly minded lads when they were serving a short prison sentence for theft whilst still young. On release, they all kept in touch, frequently drinking together into the early hours. It was at one of these sessions that they began a plan to move from their frequent petty theft to something on a far larger scale.

Unsuspecting casinos were their target.

They checked into Antonio's hotel and made themselves comfortable. They initially planned to stay just a few weeks, but when they realised there was not just one casino to visit but two, their stay eventually turned out to be four months in total. During that time, they were very busy indeed. They visited both casinos regularly and, little by little defrauded one of them of many thousands. They did it cleverly, losing small amounts at first to gain the confidence of the management. Gradually, the stakes increased and the tables were turned in their favour by the use of devious tricks that were never seen. They were truly skilled at their evil game.

They relatively quickly were able to bankrupt the smaller of Antonio's casinos. With the time he had spent with both his wife, whom he adored and his busy hotel, he had taken his eye off the ball with his casinos. He had trusted his managers who, it turned out, were unfortunately no match for this gang. They had bled him dry. Consequently, this first casino was now close to worthless. The brothers were then able to buy it for a song, knowing that once it returned to profitability, as it now would, its value would soar. The gang put in a manager they could trust to manage it for the short term. They then left town, leaving behind a massive unpaid hotel bill. They left, but only temporarily.

Antonio licked his wounds for a while, but eventually, satisfied himself with his second casino, his profitable hotel, and his lovely wife, Kokee. She had many talents and, whilst managing the hotel, was still able to find time for her other interests. The main one was wedding planning. After arranging everything for their own, she had learnt a great deal to add to her natural creative abilities. She arranged many of them. Not only were they lucrative work, but of course, also brought significant business to their hotel. Antonio again settled back down to a contented lifestyle.

Unknown to him, the earlier card shark gang had returned, not satisfied with just one small casino. They had set their sights higher. They wanted his larger one too, and they knew how to get it.

They checked into another hotel in a different neighbourhood and made their plans. Day by day, week by week, they began sucking his remaining casino dry. By the time Antonio realised that history was repeating itself, it was too late for recovery.

He went to the police and explained all that had happened, firstly to his smaller casino and now, to his larger one too. They made a gesture at investigating what was going on but didn't really understand what system the brothers were employing nor did they see anything illegal to put a finger on. They told Antonio he had no real case against them and that they didn't plan to look into the complaint any further. Antonio was now powerless to do anything but slowly watch this casino going bankrupt. They had achieved their goal in a remarkably short time. His casino business was now bankrupt. He had lost it all in a cruel, illegal scam by unscrupulous thieves.

Together with Kokee, he considered their financial position. They put their heads together to try to find a way forward. They had the hotel and a little in savings. Just about enough to survive but not enough to heal their deep wounds; wounds caused by such vile injustice. It was Kokee's idea. It is fair to say that she was the brains behind the plan; the plan of establishing Pathways.

It required substantial capital, some money they had and some that they were able to borrow against their very profitable hotel. So, they were now set to get moving with this mission.

These eight people on their way to Guatemala on board the small Gulfstream aircraft were going to be the solution to their plight. Not that they yet knew the work they had ahead of them. They all had problems to hide, and problems to run away from, and Antonio and Kokee knew everything about their past and their reasons for shortly staying at their hotel. It was this intimate information that made their plan possible. They felt confident of its success. For many weeks, they had been planning for the arrival of these recruits. Recruits who would surely be willing missionaries! Once they had arrived, they would have little choice.

For the first time in quite a while, he and Kokee felt that they held all the cards.

Chapter 11

On board the plane, Peter Andrews introduced himself to George Middleton, sitting next to him. They had little in common, George being exactly twice Peter's age at sixty-eight.

Without giving reasons for their journeys, they talked about their pasts.

"I am an electronics engineer," Peter told George. "I lived in Reading and worked in Bracknell until a few weeks ago. I decided I wanted a fresh start, so here I am. How about you?"

"Nothing like that. I am just coming up to my sixty-ninth birthday and have been retired for the past seven years. I was a plumber for most of my life," he went on to say.

"Were you ever married?" Peter asked.

"Yes, I was, but now separated." He didn't want to divulge more at this stage. "And you, Peter, are you married?"

"No, not now, I was, but got divorced several years ago." They went on to ask each other a few questions about what their future plans were. The responses were guarded on both sides. Both had to admit that there really were few in their minds! At this stage, it was becoming obvious that they both had a past to hide. Pasts they were not yet ready to reveal.

Angela McHaig, sitting across the small aisle from Joanna Crawley, introduced herself. She said, "Hello, pleased to get to know you. My name is Angela, and I am a retired singer!"

"Wow," she replied. "I am amazed you could be retired, you look far too young. I'm Joanna. I have been working as a model, mainly in and around London." Angela then went on to explain that she had become bored with the same routines night after night and wanted a change. Like others, she clearly didn't want to add more about her past or reasons for being on this flight; at least not at this early stage. She then told Joanna that, looking at her, she could see why she was a model. She said she could see that she was tall, slim and very attractive. She tried to hide that in truth, she fancied her like hell! Joanna was flattered and liked what she heard. She certainly didn't spot what Angela was thinking.

Jonathan and his son, Michael, sat quietly opposite each other, exchanging glances and occasionally looking around this small plane, but said nothing.

Wan Lung sat alone in the last pair of seats. He kept running this whole scenario through his mind. Other than the fact that they now knew they were all heading to Guatemala on this very small plane, he knew nothing more. Guatemala was somewhere he had never been nor knew much about.

The limit of his knowledge was that it was close to Mexico and Spanish speaking. A language he knew nothing of other than 'si' for yes and 'gracia' for thank you! He guessed their currency wouldn't be Euros, but didn't know what it was. Frankly, all seven passengers, along with the pilot, Matt, knew nothing of what was ahead at all.

The small plane noisily ran down the runway and very quickly took to the air. The climb was not only loud but was rather bumpy too. In addition, everything on board buzzed and shook for several minutes during the climb. Small planes like this one are a very different experience from the huge plane they were in just a short while ago. After about twenty minutes, the plane levelled off and began a rather quieter cruise. Some of the passengers helped themselves to drinks from the fridge in the small galley at the rear of the plane. Eventually, they all settled back and either relaxed, dozed or actually went into deep sleep. After all, they had four hours or so ahead with nothing to do and travel so far had been exhausting.

On the tiny flight deck, Matt was concentrating on his job of safely flying this small plane. It brought back memories as this was the kind of plane he trained on and had started his flying career with.

It was a huge contrast to the massive 777 he was flying just a few hours before! As there is always much to do when flying small planes like this, ones without the many automated systems the larger ones have, Matt was kept busy and the four hours passed quickly and without incident. He contacted the control tower at Guatemala City Airport for landing information. He was promptly given the coordinates and clearance to land at will. He advised his passengers to fasten their seatbelts in readiness for landing. This announcement awakened some of them from their sleep.

Guatemala has a diverse landscape. There are huge and beautiful forest areas that are breathtaking, but also mountainous areas. There are some twenty-seven volcanoes, three of which are still technically considered active. These are all over two thousand metres in height. The highest of these is the Volcan Tajumulco in the southwest. Rising four thousand two hundred and twenty metres above sea level, it is the highest peak in Central America.

Once awake, all passengers marvelled at this beautiful landscape as they descended towards the airport. Matt brought the plane around and lined up with the runway. The landing was smooth and uneventful.

"Welcome to Guatemala City Airport. We will disembark in just a few moments after I have brought your plane closer to the terminal building." True to his word, they were inside the building and ready to leave by bus just fifteen minutes later.

They were greeted by Kokee, ready with a minibus to transport them to their hotel. This bus was the one owned by Antonio and Kokee and was the one frequently used for this run when taking care of their normal hotel guests. Their final destination was to be Zacapa, some eighty kms (fifty miles) away. They were just a couple of hours away from being 'home'.

Once Kokee and Antonio had decided on this plan, they had spent many weeks planning and anticipating this arrival. A great deal depended upon it being successful for this lovely couple, a couple who had put everything into it. Not least of which was a considerable sum, much of it currently on loan from their bank!

Other than all the transport arrangements, the plane diversion, the Gulfstream plane and the minibus, much had been going on in their hotel behind the scenes. They had set aside a sizeable area of their hotel as a private casino, an area dedicated to a training school.

In addition, a Spanish teacher was hired on a twelve-week contract to further execute their plan.

These guests still had no idea of what they would be getting for this escape, nor what was going to be required of them at all. What they, however, all knew was that they were free of what they had each left behind. At least for the moment.

As they each boarded the minibus, they were required to give up their passports, driving licences, their phones, and any bank traces such as credit cards, prior to being able to check in to their accommodation. They all had concerns about this but were assured that it was a condition of moving any further forward. They were assured that this was in their interests and that all would shortly be explained to them on arrival at their destination.

They spent the next couple of hours chatting with each other and enjoying the lovely landscape. Just over two hours later, they arrived at their new home; the Pathways Hotel and Restaurant. This was Kokee and Antonio's hotel. They were shown to their rooms and asked to refresh and meet together in the lounge one hour later, where some of the plan was to be revealed. The hotel and rooms were on a four-star standard, perfectly comfortable and spacious. All rooms had a comfortable double bed as well as a separate single in addition. The en-suite in each had a shower rather than a bath.

There were tea and coffee-making facilities and a small mini-bar with a selection of soft drinks provided. They really were trying hard to make these new guests feel welcome and comfortable during their stay at Pathways.

Whilst still not yet knowing what the plan ahead was, they couldn't complain about the quality of their accommodation.

Chapter 12

Located on the shore of Lake Atitlan, near the Mayan village of Santiago Atitlan, this lovely hotel and well-established restaurant has been open since 1991. An eighteen-roomed hotel with a variety of room styles, all with hand-carved Central American cedar doors. Each tastefully decorated with local oil paintings and weavings.

Everyone was more than happy to have finished travelling and all were looking forward to something to eat and drink, followed by some sleep, as it was getting late and they were tired after such a gruelling journey. One by one, they all assembled in the lounge as requested. Here, they were delighted to find a well-stocked bar and were offered anything they wished to drink. All gladly accepted, most taking a large stiff one!

Antonio and Kokee both entered the room after a few minutes and introduced themselves. Antonio explained, "My name is Antonio and this is Kokee, my wife. I am sure that you will recognise her as your bus driver earlier! We are the owners of the 'Pathways Hotel', at which you are most welcome. We hope you will all be comfortable here for what will probably be some time; whilst undertaking a mission for us. All details of it, its reason, and our plans for your future following its completion, will be explained to you tomorrow."

"Rest assured that your fully inclusive stay in our hotel will be at no cost to you whatsoever. However, you will be required to work for us during your stay. To earn your keep, so to speak. In addition, you will all be given some cash each week to spend as you wish; pocket money you may perhaps consider it to be! Please go through to our dining room and choose from the menu we have prepared for you. After what we hope will be a good relaxing night's sleep, please all meet together again in the lounge before your breakfast, at 8 am sharp. Enjoy your evening, our new friends." A brief round of applause followed.

As they all moved towards the dining room, each wondered what kind of work was in store for them and what would be their future after its completion.

They were probably also wondering what was to become of their passports, their mobile phones, and their bank cards/information. They surely felt their identities had been taken away from them! They could only hope to have answers to these and many other questions that they had the following morning.

In the dining room, they found there was just one round table laid for eight; there were no other diners. This was because the hotel had been purposefully closed to await just these eight special guests. The room was large enough to seat fifty or more diners at a more normal time. It was most elegant. It had large arched windows facing the lake and the San Pedro Volcano. The roof was supported by massive stone columns. It was certainly elegant and comfortable in every way.

Antonio and Kokee had deliberately put them all on the same table, one they would share in the weeks and months ahead. It was done this way so that they all could get to know each other and share a common purpose. The purpose that they were all there for.

To facilitate this initial intimate time together, each had a name place and also a first name badge. Antonio had ensured they would each get to know the others by name. Peter spoke first. He said, "We are clearly all here for our own reasons, reasons we do not need to share if we don't choose. However, I think to begin the process of getting acquainted, we should at least each properly introduce ourselves by giving some background of our past or career."

George spoke next. "I agree. I am happy to start, and then perhaps we can go around the table in a clockwise direction?" There were nods of acceptance of this idea, so he began. "My name is George, as you can see from this garish name tag on my shirt. I would like to say to begin, that Peter's idea to give our backgrounds is good, but we should all be mindful that we do not need to give more information than we feel comfortable with; after all, we all have a right to any privacy we want. However, we all have a fresh start here, so honesty should surely be essential. All we do say must be factual." There were murmurs of acceptance around the table, which could clearly be heard by everyone.

"Ok, so here goes. I'm George and am sixty-nine years of age. As an aside and in a nervous, perhaps humorous way, all please note that my seventieth birthday is in just three weeks, so do get ready with cards and gifts for my special celebration day coming up!" Laughter rang around the room at this comment. The mood in the room was certainly beginning to lighten as they all settled into this new environment. "I was born and then raised for my early years in the docks area of Liverpool. My parents were not impressed with the local schools and therefore relocated to Chester, where they felt I would stand a better chance of a superior education."

"In actual fact, it didn't turn out all that well, in that I eventually achieved little in the way of qualifications. My only claim to fame there was that I became a commensurate rugby player and played for the county. On leaving school, I made a good friend of a well-qualified plumber who took me under his wing; he taught me the trade. I had many years of experience of rushing out to emergency water leaks, those that always seemed to happen at weekends for some reason! These were our favourites as the fee was always much higher then."

"When he retired, I took over the business. I didn't marry until I was thirty-eight, having stayed footloose and fancy-free until then. During thirty years of marriage, we drifted apart, partly due to the hours I worked and also as the years went by, we seemed to have less and less in common. We never had any children, as I never wanted them. This was a bone of contention, as my wife would have liked them. We eventually separated and I retired two years ago with sufficient cash due to a lucky windfall. I am here now looking for a new future, a fresh start."

Most must have thought this was a thorough explanation of George's background, although some wondered why he took this leap for a new life.

He had given no reason for doing so. Most wondered, would he eventually divulge this omitted piece of his history?

At this point, George suggested that having got the ball rolling, they order their food choices and continue these introductions afterwards. He also pointed out that a breathing space would give everyone time to collect their thoughts and prepare their introductions. They agreed and all studied the dinner menu choices.

It was a wide selection. A choice of three starters, three main courses, and three deserts in addition. On the table were also red and white house wines to choose from, along with bottled water. There were starter choices of prawn cocktail, avocado pear, or mussels. The mains were fish and chips, beef stroganoff or a vegetable curry. Finally, desserts were ice cream, apple pie and cream or cheese and biscuits. Kokee had obviously made an effort to ensure they had familiar British food on the menu; at least for their first night in a country that most likely was unfamiliar to most, if not to all of them.

The menu advised the diners at the bottom of the page that there would be a different menu each day. All ordered their choices and talked amongst themselves, whilst their food was being prepared. After just a few minutes, their food arrived and they all hungrily tucked into their dinners. Once all had been eaten, they relaxed to enjoy their coffee, tea or liqueurs; whilst the plates and the table were cleared. Now it was time to properly introduce themselves. Peter was next seated around this large round table.

"So, this is me, I'm Peter Andrews. I am thirty-five years old and a retired director of an electronics company in Bracknell, Berkshire. I was forced to leave for personal reasons, reasons that I do not wish to reveal at the moment. Since my divorce several years ago, when my wife kept our house, I had been renting a flat in Reading. I was ready for a fresh start, so I took this journey. One of my passions is motorcycling. I unfortunately had to leave my cherished bikes behind, three of them. Hopefully, my friend will sell them for me, as I have requested. We all are going to spend much time with each other over the coming months, so I am sure we will gradually learn more about each other. Thank you for listening to my little story!"

He then sat down, clearly having given as much background information as he felt comfortable with at this time.

Joanna Crawley stood up next and rather nervously introduced herself. "At just twenty-six years of age, I suspect I am the youngest here! After leaving school, with little in the way of academic qualifications to my name, I decided to attempt some kind of modelling career by working for a catalogue clothes-selling company. This went quite well, although the wages were rather poor. Eventually, I was approached by a men's magazine and asked to participate in photograph sessions, the payment for which was generous. This then led me to night club work, which, although even better paid, was not what I wanted to do. I just wasn't comfortable with it. After saving enough money, I decided on this new start, so here I am!"

Wan Lung followed Joanna. He was clearly Chinese and on occasions, his accent, coupled with broken English, made him rather difficult to understand. "Hello, everybody, I am Wan; Wan Lung from China. I am forty-seven years of age and was born and raised in Shantou, a bustling town about three hundred kilometres north-east of Hong Kong. I lived on the coast of the South China Sea. I never married and indeed never felt interested in women. Instead, I pursued a business of selling electronic equipment to local people who failed to understand it the way I did. I liked my work but felt restrained by so many regulations and specific local ways of business. Also, the returns were small."

"I could see a far better opportunity was probably possible somewhere else in Europe. So, ten years ago, I emigrated to the United Kingdom. There, I set up and executed the most successful business, which made me a very comfortable living. Unfortunately, I failed to understand the tax implications and got deeply in trouble with your customs and excise people. They made my business suddenly look unprofitable and my life most difficult, so I decided to start anew somewhere else and leave these customs people behind. So, I did and here I am!"

Next around this large round table was Jonathan Clarke and his son, Michael. "Well, a very good evening to you all. I am Jonathan and this is my son, Michael. I am fifty-three years old and Michael is just twenty-five. I am a boxer who was forced to retire due to a bad fight defeat that left me with a blood clot on my brain. It is unlikely to be life-threatening if not disturbed, or so the medical experts say maybe to comfort me! I don't know, but for certain, further fighting would be not only reckless but likely very dangerous. So, having made a good bounty for the many fights I did win, we decided to start a new life here."

"Michael was of a similar frame of mind, having few prospects back in the UK and being rather close to his dad. We are not sure what we are looking for yet, as is probably true for some of you too I would guess. I just hope we will all get on well together and be happy here, carrying out the work being set for us, whatever it is going to be."

Now, there were just two people left yet to formally introduce themselves. Angela was next. She stood and spoke in a broad Scottish accent."I'm Angela McHaig. If you can't guess from my name, you surely will from my accent. I am a native of Scotland! I am a professional singer hailing from a wee suburb of Dundee. I don't feel the need to declare my age, or any of my statistics at this moment as I feel a bit shy this evening. You may find it hard to understand my lack of confidence, seeing as I am a singer. Well, I can explain. On stage being behind a microphone is a comfort zone for me, something I am used to."

"It is nowhere as daunting as addressing you all in this way. Please, forgive my initial shyness, I am sure I will emerge from my shell in the coming days and weeks." With that, and blushed cheeks, she sat down again.

Last to speak was Matt. "Bonus noches, amigos. My name is Matt. No, I am not Spanish, just able to speak a little. You all will, of course, know I have been your pilot since we left Heathrow on our first ill-fated flight. I have been privy to this plan so far, a key part of the travel arrangements that got us here. However, from here on, I know no more than any of you. I was just needed for the travel arrangements. I worked at many small jobs to save enough money to train as a junior pilot for Ryanair. After a few years, I was able to gain a promotion and a rather better-paid job as a co-pilot for British Airways, flying large planes such as the one we all started out on from Heathrow."

"I am thirty-four years of age and wanted to see far more of the world than British Airways could offer me with a very limited destination timetable. Also, it was far from a glamorous job. All you see are the four walls of a hotel room for one night. Friends used to ask me, in an envious way, what is San Francisco like? I had to point out to them that, even after piloting planes there several times, I had seen nothing of the city. Not even the famous landmark of the Golden Gate Bridge, except from the air! When the mission we have all been recruited for is complete, I plan to travel extensively. I particularly want to see Thailand." With that, he sat down.

Once these introductions were complete, an ordeal for some, they all felt more relaxed. One by one, they then all retired to their rooms and their most welcome comfy beds.

Most probably lay awake pondering their past and wondering about their future. Tomorrow was, after all, going to be the first day of the rest of their lives.

Joanna lay awake for a long time. She found herself thinking back on her whole life. She was born in Slough to middle-class parents. Her father worked as a senior security manager at Heathrow Airport, often working shifts and late nights. Her mother looked after their home and her older sister, Julia. The two girls, just three years apart in age, were both very competitive. As they matured in their teens, they constantly compared each other's bodies. Joanna really bloomed and developed a generous bust, which earned her much attention from a lot of boys, far more so than her sister.

Julia, she remembered, was always jealous of the attention she got. Julia was the more academic and achieved by far the better exam results. Whilst she went on to train as a lawyer in a successful practice, Joanna lost her way a bit and eventually fell back on her attractive looks and figure. Minor modelling contracts came quite easily but were not as lucrative as she wanted. It was the move to the lap dancing club and its seedy side businesses that were her downfall.

The politician she started 'seeing' was generous and not hard work in any way. She did know, however, that he had many enemies, due mainly to his extreme views on homosexuality.

She was initially shocked when she learnt that he had been murdered, but in hindsight, it probably was not so surprising. What was an even bigger shock was that she had been singled out as a prime suspect. That was what had brought about her journey to Guatemala. She gradually fell asleep.

Jonathan and his son, Michael, were sharing a spacious suite and sat at their coffee table and talked well into the early hours. They were already planning a future for them both, a future that could possibly take them away from this place. This was what they wanted, but they realised that without new passports, they wouldn't be able to get far. They would have to toe the line and bide their time. On this, they both agreed.

Chapter 13

At 8 am, most were already assembled in the lounge as requested, but there was one absentee; there was no sign of Angela. Kokee and Antonio were there already and awaiting their guests. They had much to tell them.

After fifteen minutes had transpired, there was still no sign of her. Kokee went up to Angela's room and knocked the door firmly. After a few moments, she appeared in a dressing gown rubbing her eyes. She had seriously overslept and could only apologise for her tardy behaviour. She promised she could be down in less than thirty minutes. Kokee went back to the lounge and explained to the others. Most realised that having seen her drinking a great deal of wine the night before, the oversleep was the direct result of that. Despite the tea, coffee and orange juice available for them for the next thirty minutes or so, few had little sympathy for the delay they would all now experience. She hadn't made a very good first impression on the rest of the group.

Thirty-five minutes later, a dishevelled Angela appeared rather humbly. She apologised, although this cut little ice with the rest who would rather have got this meeting over and then been able to partake of their breakfast.

"Well, Kokee and I hope you all enjoyed your dinner last night and that you slept well. I suspect you did after such a long and tedious journey! We have an important mission for you all, which may take some time. When accomplished, you will be free to go anywhere you choose with fresh identities. More on how we will assist you later. We will explain the mission and how you are going to accomplish it after you have had your breakfast."

"Firstly, however, some logistics for you. As I explained earlier, you will all be given some money each week to spend as you please. This will be just until we can get bank accounts opened for you here. You will have both Saturday and Sunday as free time. You may choose to explore the area a little whilst here for example. Taxis are cheap and plentiful should you need them. We can call one for you at any time. Monday to Friday, you will be under our tuition from 9 in the morning until about 5 in the afternoon. That time will be spent partly learning to speak Spanish to a reasonable standard and partly to become experts at gambling. More to the point, you will become experts at winning!"

"To facilitate this, we have set up our own training casino in a room upstairs, a place that you haven't yet seen."

There were several protests and complaints voiced by some. Angela said, "What about things we need now? I will shortly be needing some items from a pharmacy."

Antonio replied, "Today is Thursday. On Saturday, you will be free to go into town and purchase anything you need; in the meantime, if you do need anything, just ask Kokee and she will get it for you." This seemed to satisfy them all for the moment. This initial meeting then closed and they all went through to the breakfast room.

Here, they found a self-service selection of hot and cold food, typical of a four-star hotel. There was also plenty of tea, coffee, and fruit juices to choose from. They again were seated at the same round table that they had used for their dinner the previous night. Their name place labels were still in their original positions.

Now, without any doubt, all were grateful to have escaped from the problems each had left behind in the UK, however, they all had concerns as to what they had enrolled themselves into. They were mindful that not only had they all paid substantial money to get this far, but that they had effectively given up their identities, as well as access to their banks and contact with anyone back home in the UK.

George spoke to Peter, who was seated next to him. "Do you have any real idea as to why we have been recruited in this way? After all, we have each clearly paid out a sizeable sum and this whole project is costing these folks a great deal of money."

Peter replied, "I only know what you do, but it seems we are going to set out to earn money by gambling, presumably at a casino. I don't know if what will be expected of us will even be legal!"

Joanna sitting next to Peter clearly couldn't fail to hear this conversation. "I too am puzzled as to understand how I will be of use; assuming we have to speak Spanish and know how to gamble. I know nothing of either and I certainly don't know what a poker face is!"

Peter replied, "I am confident that Antonio and Kokee know what they are doing. They have clearly demonstrated intelligence and very efficient planning so far. We must just have faith in them with the knowledge that we will each be given new futures once we complete this mission."

Chapter 14

In the UK, Reading police were on the hunt. They were seeking a certain individual known as Peter Andrews. After causing the death of a woman and child in an appalling drink drive accident, he had apparently vanished. He had failed to attend his court appearance to face trial.

They first visited his home. No answer there. Their next port of call was his workplace. They spoke directly to his managing director, Graham Deval. He quickly confirmed that Peter had registered for a two-week holiday, telling the board that he was going to San Francisco. Graham, in further discussions with the police, was able to confirm that they knew nothing of his accident and the outstanding court appearance. On the day of the accident, it had been recorded that he called in sick with the flu the following morning. That was the day, following the accident, when he went to see his new lawyer.

The police then checked with both airlines operating flights to San Francisco in the few days that followed the accident. It didn't take long to find out that he was booked onto the British Airways Wednesday Flight BA0285 to San Francisco.

The Reading detectives had now traced him to his flight but there, they became puzzled.

Two of them flew to San Francisco and talked to both the BA staff and the immigration officials, only to further deepen the mystery as to Peter's whereabouts. It quickly became clear that, whilst he had boarded the plane at Heathrow, he never arrived in the USA along with the other passengers.

The two detectives soon ascertained that the plane had diverted to Pinal Airpark in Arizona for a few hours before flying on to its final planned destination in the USA. They then went to this stop off airstrip to interrogate the staff there as to what could have happened to this elusive, and much-wanted, passenger.

The airport manager, Jim Petty, was the main person they questioned. They spent a considerable time with him but learnt little. It quickly became clear that, whilst they checked all passengers off the plane, they failed to repeat the checks of seeing them back on it again. Peter had seemingly ended his journey there. The two detectives, Jeff Taylor and William Thompson, then talked to the local taxi firms serving the area. They showed Peter's picture to the drivers in the hope that one of them would recognise him. There was, however, no positive identification from any driver.

They then spent several days visiting all local hotels, boarding houses, and rentable accommodations trying to locate Peter. All with no success. He had simply vanished, as of course was his intention. They subsequently returned to the UK, empty-handed and most frustrated. Having already checked both his mobile phone calls and his recent credit card transactions, they simply still had nothing to go on. Where he had gone to was a mystery.

The Middlesex police were busy too. They were independently looking for a certain Jonathan Clarke. He had very seriously injured a youth in a drunken fight. Actually, unknown to Jonathan, the injuries were so severe that the youth was eventually diagnosed with permanent brain damage. There had been a date set for the trial, but whilst on bail, Jonathan had run away. Like Peter Andrews, the police traced him to the San Francisco flight.

They didn't travel to the USA, instead, they chose to set up a video conference call with the immigration officials at the airport. They quickly confirmed that neither Jonathan nor his son were on the plane as it landed in San Francisco. They did, however, give Jason Murdoch, the senior investigating officer, two useful pieces of information.

Firstly, that the plane had experienced a problem with one of the crew and had been diverted briefly to the Pinal Airstrip in Arizona, and secondly, this was the second recent enquiry they had received from UK police about another missing passenger. They gave the contact details of the Reading police who were seeking this other person. The individual we know as Peter Andrews. Rather than repeat the work already done by the Reading detectives, Jason decided to contact them to see what they had learnt. This looked like an opportunity for these two forces to join and work together with a common mission.

This turned out to be a good thing as there had been friction between the two forces in the past. Berkshire constabulary and Middlesex constabulary were the subject of much criticism a couple of years earlier when a rapist had committed copycat crimes in both areas but the two forces never shared their information; neither of the crimes nor the findings of the assaults. The result was that it took far longer to bring the man to justice than it should have done. Whilst the considerable delays ensued, he committed two more offences. Offences that could have been prevented if the two forces had worked together. Each blamed the other but the truth was that each had different databases which were not compatible.

What did come out of it was positive. Almost all forces in Southern England got together and invested in a common system that was transparent to each. This was a considerable investment but proved to be well worthwhile in solving many future crimes.

Jason contacted his counterpart at the Reading police station and set up a meeting for the following day. He met with Jeff Taylor and compared notes. They had similar information but there were two people that could assist and yet had not been contacted by either force. These were the two pilots. Jason took the task of pursuing this line of enquiry. He spoke with British Airways and quickly ascertained something interesting. Namely, that whilst the original captain of the flight had returned home after feeling unwell, the co-pilot simply vanished after the plane landed at Pinal Airstrip, just like the other two who also had done so. British Airways had no idea where he had gone.

They established that his name was Matt Dunbar. After circulating his name to other forces in the UK, it soon became apparent that he was also wanted, this time by Essex police, for a series of sex offences. So now, at least three people who vanished from this flight partway were all wanted by the police. Jeff Taylor again spoke with British Airways and discovered that there had been an anomaly concerning passenger numbers.

The difference was that twelve fewer passengers finally disembarked in San Francisco than had checked in at Heathrow. The wanted co-pilot made the thirteenth suspicious person. Two were quickly accounted for as Jayne and Alan Wilson who were removed from the plane before it even left London. They were charged and subsequently convicted of robbing a bank and were currently behind bars serving lengthy prison sentences. Three others were arrested whilst delayed overnight at a hotel near the airport. This was the Singh family who were found guilty of drug dealing and also given prison terms.

So, now, there were eight people missing under suspicious circumstances. Four of which were so far identified. It didn't take long for the two police forces, working together, to establish the names of the other four. As we know, they were Joanna Crawley, Wan Lung, George Middleton, and Angela McHaig. Eventually, after several weeks of research, they found out why three of them were on the run. All were wanted by police forces for various crimes. However, one still was a mystery, this was George Middleton. His wife confirmed he had just left with no reason having been given. Despite extensive checks with all of the other UK police forces, they could find no reason to explain his disappearance. It seemed he, unlike the others, had committed no crime.

Chapter 15

Maria, George Middleton's wife, had a shock when the Wednesday post arrived. There were two envelopes, one addressed to her, the other to her absconded husband. She opened hers first. It was the usual monthly bank statement; they never learnt to fully do their banking online and were stuck in the past with paper by post.

Her statement contained no surprises; only the usual pension in and shopping out. The current balance was just £427.31. For the first time in her married life, she opened her husband's post. She nearly fainted. It showed a credit of £6,039,216. OVER £6 MILLION! It was swiftly followed by a debit of the same amount, payable to an unnamed overseas account.

She sat down before she fainted and fell. At first, she could think of no reason to explain this massive windfall. They had no wealthy relatives and, to her knowledge, were not pending beneficiaries of anyone's will. On pondering the possibilities, her only conclusion was that this could have been a lottery win. She knew he did occasionally do the weekly draw but had never taken any interest in it.

This, of course, now explained his motive for leaving her. He had simply run off with the money. This was money that they should surely have enjoyed together. Indeed, she now began to think about her legal entitlement to at least a share of it. She phoned Jeff Taylor, the detective who had been to see her the previous week. She told him what she had found. Jeff told her he would visit later that day to both see and take a copy of, this bank statement.

At just after 4 pm that afternoon, he rang her doorbell. She answered it promptly and invited him in. She was in tears. She told him just how upset she had been ever since reading his goodbye note and that this news, whilst offering some kind of explanation, only upset her further. He took a photo of the bank statement and promised that he would look into it further by visiting the bank concerned. He then suggested she also take it to a lawyer as she would have a good case for half of the money, particularly if they divorced.

It would, however, depend upon being able to locate him and also the overseas bank holding the money. He warned her it would certainly take time but it was something she certainly should get started on right away. He left having decided to make an appointment with the manager of their local bank to see what could be found out from there.

Jeff made an appointment to see William Spinks, the manager of the bank concerned. Three days later, he was in his office. The meeting was brief and fairly unproductive. All William could tell him was that it was a credit from the National Lottery for a recent win and that the money was duly transferred in full to an unnamed offshore account, with no trace by them being possible. This was pretty much what was already known. He did point out that the account was still open with a small balance and, under the circumstances, should probably be closed. He did explain that, without a court injunction, this could only be done by George himself.

As divorce was likely to be the next course of action, closing the account with a court injunction seemed likely at some point in the future. He thanked the manager for his assistance and left to inform Maria of his findings and also of the manager's advice. This, he did a few days later. She was not surprised and agreed that pursuing a divorce was her best course of action. Finding George and then the money would clearly be challenging, however.

Back in Guatemala, George had no idea what his wife had found out; he was blissfully unaware that she was on his trail. He hadn't considered the monthly statement that had duly arrived at their house.

He'd assumed, after visiting the bank in person and making the transfer, that the communication would end there. How wrong he was!

After the group of eight had finished their breakfast, they were instructed by Kokee to go through to the adjoining conference room. Antonio was already there waiting for them.

He stated, "As I told you earlier, we have a very important mission for you all. With your help, we are going to regain two casinos that were stolen from Kokee and me by an unscrupulous gang. I don't plan or need to explain to you how it happened, only how together we will achieve this task. I already indicated to you that it would involve learning basic Spanish and becoming an expert gambler. These two things we will achieve together in the coming weeks and perhaps even months."

The feelings amongst the group were clearly mixed. Some were just going along with the plan, perhaps even relishing the tasks that were being outlined. Others were sceptical and even not feeling particularly cooperative. He went on, "During the next few days, either Kokee or I will go with each of you in turn to visit a very close friend of ours in the town. Here, you will be able to sign up for a new name, a new passport; an identity that cannot be traced."

"This is on the pre-requisite that none of you make any contact whatsoever with your past life. This is vital for you all to fully escape your past. Once this is all complete, each of you will come with me to open up your own new bank account. We will arrange for any monies you have left behind to be discretely transferred. When they have been prepared, your new passports will be held by us and eventually released to you upon completion of your work. You will then be free to truly begin your new lives."

He sat down and invited questions.

Peter Andrews spoke first. He said, "I cannot speak on behalf of the whole group but we have been talking amongst ourselves and it would seem there is much we all need to know, understand, and learn. However, I think it likely we would all like to listen and go along with your plans for the moment."

He then looked around to see what support or otherwise he had for this statement. The positive murmurs around the group and the visible body language made it fairly clear that they were broadly in agreement with him.

The group had not elected a leader or any kind of spokesperson, nor had they expressed any desire to have one, however, it was becoming clear that if there was going to be such a person, then Peter was probably the prime candidate for the job.

No one else spoke, so Antonio did. "Right, please come with me through to our small home casino training room."

They followed him through into a lovely well-furnished room. It really had the look and feel of a mini-casino.

"Firstly, we must ascertain which of you have past gambling experience with the particular card game known as Black Jack; variants of it are sometimes also known as 21s or Pontoon."

After a few minutes of discussion among them, it became clear that the group was evenly divided. Four had some past experience, or at least understood the basics of the game. Four knew nothing about it whatsoever. "Well, we have some work to do", Kokee said from behind a gambling table.

The four with some knowledge were Peter Andrews, Joanna Crawley, Wan Lung, and Matt Dunbar.

These four were invited to sit around the arc-shaped table on stools, all facing Kokee, who was clearly going to be the dealer, the croupier. The other four were asked to each stand behind a player, ensuring they had a good view of the table.

Each of the four players was given a hundred plastic tokens to play with. Kokee explained, "We are going to run through a few games during the next couple of hours. We will critique and discuss all wins and losses. Those who have never played should quite quickly pick up the basics of the game, but more importantly, all will gradually learn how to win, not just how to play. A professional casino usually uses at least four or five packs of cards, all shuffled together, but for these early training days, we will use just two. You will shortly see why."

She then dealt one card to each player and one to herself, all face-up. She then gave each of the four players a second card, again face-up and laid, so all cards were visible. She gave herself a second card too, but hers was placed under her first card and its value concealed. Her first face-up card was a queen.

She went on to ask the first player if they wanted another card. It was Peter. He had a king and a five, so a value of 15. The dealer was showing a queen and an unknown card. Peter chose to 'stand', declining another card. She moved to the next player, Joanna. She had a ten and an eight. She also chose to 'stand' on this score of 18. She then turned to Wan, the third player. He had a seven and a four, a total of 11. He requested another card, feeling confident. He received an eight. At 19, this was a good hand; although, he had quietly hoped for a face card to make 21. Matt came last. He had a seven and a five and requested another card hoping for a nine or less. She dealt him a queen…so 22 was a bust.

The dealer then turned over her hidden card to display a three. She took a third card, which was a four. Her total was now 17. She announced, "I will pay 18s and over." With 15, Peter had lost his bet. With 18, Joanna won hers. With 19, Wan also won his hand. Matt had already lost his.

They then had a discussion as to any wrongs and rights of the decisions made. In this case, it was agreed that all had done the right thing. Peter's 15 was not good, but the odds of beating a dealer showing a 10 were slim. Indeed, had he taken the next card, it would have been an eight, as Wan found out. He would, therefore, have well exceeded the needed 21 and lost in any event.

Matt had little choice but to call for another card, as he knew that 12 would almost certainly have lost. The catch, however, was that a lot of cards have a value of 10, so the odds were not really in his favour either way.

During the next two hours, they played many hands. In the end, only Wan managed a small improvement on his initial fund of one hundred tokens by retiring with sixteen more. All the others lost heavily and, as is usually the case playing with beginners, the dealer cleaned up!

They went for a thirty-minute coffee break. They used the time to have further discussions together about the rules and the outcome of the games that some had played and some had just observed.

After their break, they again resumed their original positions. Antonio explained that there were many finer details and rules of this game, but these would wait for further advanced lessons. However, he went on to try to explain the all-important odds vital to this game.

"When you are looking for, and hoping for, a low-value card, remember this. Over half of the cards in a deck are valued at seven or higher. Furthermore, about seventy per cent of them are five or more! So, unless you know what cards have gone before, the odds of the dealer giving you a card lower than a five are more than two to one against you!"

"So, the first thing to learn well are these odds. Now, you can shorten these significantly if most of the deck has already gone and you have a good memory as to what those cards were. If you really are good at memorising the cards, you will shorten the odds by having a far better idea of which cards are left. Of course, this is not too difficult with one deck of cards, but gets far more so with multiple decks in use. This will be the case in a real casino. So, this is the training and learning we will be undertaking."

During that first morning, each of them had multiple turns to play. All of them learnt a great deal about the game, its tricks and turns. Most began to improve their play substantially. It was probably true to say, they all quite enjoyed it. At about 1 pm, they stopped for a one-hour lunch break. Again, there was a good selection of food choices made available for them. They did not doubt that they were all being well looked after.

At 2 pm, they again assembled in the casino room, which had now been laid out with seating like a school classroom. They all took their seats, each wondering in anticipation as to what was to come next. Antonio explained that their afternoon sessions were to be Spanish language lessons. So now, it was his turn to be the teacher for the group for a while.

He began by explaining that these sessions were not to be intense technical learning ones. They were not going to be bothered with grammar, spelling or writing. They would merely be learning enough for basic conversation purposes, designed for them to be able to speak for themselves and also to understand others. He explained that this method had been well proven by the English when sending undercover agents into Germany during the Second World War. He then went on to outline its interesting method.

"I'm going to do this by examples. Repeat together after me…Good morning."

All repeated, "Good morning."

He then said, "Bona dia."

All repeated this, "Bona dia."

He then said, "That is how you say good morning. Write it down on your notepads, it will serve as your homework, and your bedtime reading. Now, we will repeat several times." After a while, he just said 'Good morning' and they responded 'Bona dia'. He then moved on to 'Good afternoon, Buenas tardes'. Again using the same method, repeating many times. Finally 'good evening, Buenas noches'.

They repeated just these three expressions for most of the afternoon session. They surely would not forget these now.

He told them that each day there would be more to add, but he would expect them to be able to translate and say any previously learnt expressions whenever asked.

The next day after breakfast, all went back into the casino to continue their card school sessions with Kokee. All except Peter Andrews. He went into town with Antonio to take his turn at beginning the process of creating a new identity.

They took the short drive together in Antonio's quite old-looking, red BMW. He parked in a small private car park in the town centre where he held a season pass to do so. From there, they only had a short walk together to a small café where they waited at a table for Antonio's contact. This person turned out to be more than just that, much more…he clearly was a real friend.

When Antonio was studying at college for his business degree, he met Mateo. One night after a few late study sessions, they were having a quiet drink together.

Suddenly, and without warning, two youths appeared and demanded money from the small group of students. Mateo led the response in the form of an attack on them. He was a talented judo student and knew how to defend himself. With his lead, they overcame these assailants. Antonio was very grateful for what his friend had done, so much so that they formed a bond, there and then; it was one that was to last.

Mateo arrived, a little late, and introduced himself. Peter instantly warmed to him. Antonio and Mateo talked together for some time in Spanish, apologising to Peter as they did so. Eventually, Antonio addressed Peter.

He said, "Mateo has very little English but does have a wonderful Spanish partner called Lola, who speaks not only English but also German and French. He has been a very good friend to me for many years and he has a very special skill. One that will help you more than you will probably ever fully appreciate. He is a consummate forger! He can fake any document. He has made a very lucrative living at it. He is going to give you a new identity. Name, birth certificate, bank account, driving licence, and most importantly, a new passport. This is some of what your travel fee to Pathways is paying for."

They spent the next two hours going through all the personal information that Mateo would need to do his work. It was fair to say that much of those two hours was spent laughing and joking about a recent football match in Barcelona. Finally, after Mateo had gathered all the technical information he needed, there was one more step today, photos. They, therefore, left the café and went to Mateo's studio apartment to take these important pictures.

Here, he met Lola and was very pleased with how well and kindly she greeted him. *Antonio has more to do with me yet…bank, etc., but then again over and over with all the others. This is going to be some project*, he thought. Lola took several pictures of him using a very expensive-looking Nikon camera. When the session was over, Antonio took Peter back to the hotel. He explained that they would need to return in about ten days to collect his new identity papers and passport. The plan, he explained, was then going to be opening up a local bank account in his new name, which was going to be Peter Jordon.

Antonio told him that he should keep this new surname private to only himself and his bank manager. As far as the others in the hotel, he would from now on be simply Peter, nothing more. Peter joined the others for lunch and afterwards, they all went together into their afternoon Spanish language session as usual.

That evening over dinner, Peter was asked what had transpired in the town that morning. He told them about the meeting with Antonio's friends and how the process of getting a new identity was beginning. They were pleased to hear that this vital part of their escape was underway, although they couldn't help wondering how much longer they would have to remain at this hotel.

Chapter 16

Antonio wanted to know more about what was going on at the casinos in the town centre. They were both located in a busy area populated by large stores and businesses on the west side of the city.

He knew his recruits, still undergoing training, were not yet quite ready or qualified to investigate. He also realised that he would be instantly recognised should he step into either, so he enlisted the assistance of a local friend, Danilo.

It was Danilo who had sold the Pathways Hotel to him a few years before. They shared much in common, including gambling. He made occasional visits to the town centre casinos that were the subject of Antonio's interest. He knew them both well.

He agreed to visit a couple of times in the following week and to report back to satisfy Antonio's curiosity as to how they were doing. Also to look for any vulnerabilities that could possibly be exploited by his team!

Meanwhile, both Antonio and Kokee got on with their daily work of training the eight recruits.

This training was generally going well, actually better than they had expected. There was, however, one exception. Joanna was proving to be a very slow learner, lagging well behind the rest. It quickly became clear why she went into modelling and its associated work. She was gifted with looks rather than brains! It was a harsh truth that had to be faced; she was not going to play the same roles as the others. Antonio had to find an alternative part she could play in his plans.

On Tuesday the following week, Danilo made the first visit to the smaller casino as agreed. He was surprised to see how much quieter it was than when he had last visited some three months before. It was true to say that the economic health of Guatemala had recently taken a blow with a significant rise in interest rates for borrowers from the main bank, the Banco de Guatemala. This was the one that was used by most locals purchasing their own homes or businesses.

This hike in borrowing costs had a knock-on effect on others throughout the region. Quite simply, most had reduced their spending where possible and gambling was far from a necessity. This was except for those who were seriously addicted.

Danilo moved around the different tables, sampling all of them and taking everything in as he did so.

After a few days spent on this, the smaller of the two casinos learning all he could, Danilo returned to the Pathways Hotel to report his findings to Antonio and Kokee. He told them how quiet it was and how, at one time, he could see more staff than punters. It seemed clear this casino was struggling, not making any significant money. Antonio then asked Danilo to spend a few days visiting the larger of the two casinos that he had lost. This was the one of more interest to him. He agreed and left Pathways to begin this next phase of his investigation.

Meanwhile, in the small casino, the evil brothers were holding a meeting. They had become well aware that this casino was not paying its way; not making the returns they had hoped and planned for. They together hatched a plan that they thought could solve this problem.

After checking their insurance was fully up-to-date and covered everything, the building and all of its contents, they schemed to have a catastrophic fire. They knew they could then be rid of the place and boost their bank balance considerably. They realised that its value was probably significantly less than it had been a couple of years earlier, but would nevertheless still be sufficient to suit their needs.

While Kokee and a friend together pressed on, Monday to Friday each week, with both their card school and their Spanish lessons, Antonio took all his team, one by one, into town to generate their new identities. After a couple of weeks, all were done. Each had a new name, all relevant documents and a local bank account. They all had possession of these documents, with the exception of their passports; these were held by Antonio. They would only be released when their mission was complete. He wanted to ensure they would remain at Pathways until then. Antonio and Kokee were pleased with the progress being made by their recruits and decided that in about four more weeks, they would be set to send them on missions to the casinos.

They were now beginning to see the path ahead to a successful end to their daring mission. After all, they had thought it through and planned it over many months beforehand with great precision. Surely, they deserved to beat these evil thieves. That evening, they got the team together for a meeting to inform them of the timetable for the following weeks. Each was assigned tasks at the two casinos, some gambling, some observing to continue their learning, and some attempting to actually infiltrate the owners.

Chapter 17

The brothers put their arson plan into action a couple of weeks later. They closed the small casino for redecorating. To be sure all looked genuine, they actually hired a local company to begin the work. They moved in their equipment, their paint and tools. The work began and continued for three days until late one Friday night when they packed up for the weekend. They locked up the building and vacated. They left the burglar alarm system, complete with its cameras, disarmed in order to ensure the paint odour would not trigger any of the alarm sensors, as they had been instructed by the brothers.

At about 10 pm, the two brothers made their move. They entered the casino by a rear entrance and set the necessary 'fuse' that would start the fire. This was a burning cigarette surrounded by inflammable materials such as paint brush solvent and an opened tin of paint.

They left and waited at a local restaurant where they were well-known and sure of an alibi if required. They were apprehensive as they knew there was no certainty of the total loss they needed.

An hour or so passed uneventfully, then all hell broke loose outside as two fire engines raced past, sirens blaring. They knew where they were going and were glad that clearly, a serious fire was in progress.

The fire engines arrived on the scene but access was difficult for them. The only roadway to the building was down a very narrow one-way side street. Here, at this time of night, there were always many cars parked by evening revellers frequenting the local night spots. Many parked carelessly, leaving just about enough room for a car but insufficient for these sizeable fire tenders. It, therefore, took time to get out of the hoses long enough to reach the seat of the fire. This delay was considerable, so much so that there was little left to salvage by the time they had extinguished the blaze. The entire premises were fit for nothing but demolition. Exactly what the brothers had hoped for.

After being contacted by the police who informed them of the night's events, they visited the site. Here, they were greeted by exactly what they had hoped for, a complete write-off! They left and went to lunch to celebrate. This turned out later to be rather premature.

In circumstances such as this, experts are called in to attempt to establish the cause of the fire; there always has to be a reason. Was it perhaps an electrical fault, vandalism, or some other cause? They usually get to the root of the problem. Determining this was important for both the police and of course the insurance company, which would surely be facing a significant claim. The area was quickly cordoned off by the police pending this investigation.

The first thing Juan, the chief investigator, did was to interview the brothers to ascertain what light they could throw on the possible cause. They were only able to inform them that the casino had been closed for redecoration and that the builders would have just locked up for the weekend, a short while before the blaze would have broken out. They noted the contact details of the company concerned and decided that would be their next port of call.

They met with Mateo, the owner of this decorating company later that afternoon. It was quickly ascertained that there were three men involved with this refurbishment project. After finding out what they had done that afternoon and what time they locked up for the weekend, they then asked more detailed questions about the use of any kind of flames involved in their work. This included blow lamps for paint stripping and possible smoking whilst working. Mateo was able to confirm that no paint stripping had been involved that day and that, crucially as it turned out later, only one of the three men smoked, but he was not working that day due to a family problem he had to deal with.

Juan left to get together with one of his staff to arrange an inspection of the damage the following day. This delay was needed in order to allow the debris to cool down. Also, a visit had first to be made by a building inspector to ensure entry was safe.

This clearance was given later the following afternoon. Juan and his colleague immediately began their work. They spent three painstaking days sifting through the debris looking for a possible cause. They quite quickly ruled out the likelihood of an electrical fault or of any appliance being left inadvertently switched on. They noted that there were several security cameras both inside and on the outside walls. These were all destroyed but were the kind that were transmitted to a remote server somewhere safe and secure. They then again visited Mateo to ask about this security system. He told them that the brothers had instructed that they be disabled in order to avoid paint fumes interfering with the sensors to cause a possible false alarm.

This began to arouse their suspicions of the likelihood of foul play.

The fire was big news in the town; everyone was talking about it with theories as to its cause running rife. The insurance claim, which was considerable, was promptly lodged by the brothers. It not only detailed the rebuild cost and a complete refit but also lost earnings. These were inflated, having no relevance to the casino's recent rather poor financial performance.

The insurance company, after discussions with the damage investigators, had grave doubts as to the validity of this claim. So much so that they offered a reward for information to assist their enquiries as to the circumstances that brought about the fire that night. The police were equally suspicious and even went as far as to appeal on local TV for information, asking local people to come forward with anything that could possibly assist their investigations.

It didn't take long for two young men to visit the local police station with a very useful piece of information. They were a well-known gay couple who owned a hair salon close by. They had noticed a truck that had pulled up behind the casino late that night. It had parked up on the pavement and remained there for just a few minutes before driving off at speed. They described it as dark green with a missing tail light. The police immediately realised that this description fitted a truck used by the casino's owners.

They visited them both and, on inspection of their truck, found that it did indeed have a missing tail light. They questioned them as to their whereabouts on the night of the fire. They both denied having been anywhere near the casino and cited the restaurant as their alibi. The restaurant owner confirmed that they had been dining there all evening.

The police were not satisfied or convinced and met again with the insurance assessors. They all discussed the findings of each in detail. The police were told that they too had suspicions of arson but needed more time to further their investigations at the scene.

It wasn't until ten days later that they had a breakthrough. They found a charred cigarette butt at what would have been the seat of the fire. It was beside the remains of a burnt-out plastic bottle. Forensic analysis of this bottle showed traces of paint stripper. On interrogating the decorators, it was confirmed that at no time had the paint stripper been used or left in a plastic container, it was always elsewhere, secure in a metal drum.

They now had enough evidence to confront the brothers. It was clear to the police that this was a case of arson for the purpose of insurance fraud.

Once financial records had been pulled, which showed the casino to be in serious difficulties, the police were sure they now had all the evidence they needed.

The brothers were subsequently arrested and charged with arson and attempted insurance fraud. Despite pleading not guilty, they were quickly found to be so in court two weeks later. They each received suspended prison sentences and were banned from holding gambling licences again for life. What was more painful for them, however, was the collapse of their insurance claim. They simply had lost everything.

This was music to the ears of both Antonio and Kokee. They really felt justice had been done. Karma had begun to come home. They would now redouble their efforts to regain the larger casino in the town centre. Now with the brothers out of the casino, it was likely that the day-to-day running of it would not be as efficient. This would surely open an opportunity for them. They decided that night, now was the time to start sending their team into the casino to begin their work.

Chapter 18

After breakfast the following morning, Antonio met with his trusty team of recruits. Each was then given a task to carry out.

First, he addressed Joanna. "Joanna, we want you to use your youth and attractive looks to befriend one of the managers. Your assets, coupled with the excellent Spanish you have learnt, should make this a perfect mission for you. Initially, try to get a job in the casino, most likely one of plying the punters with free drinks. Once you have achieved this, we will talk later about your key role in our overall plan."

"Wan, you next, please. Go to the casino playing a little blackjack, but in doing so, use your electronics knowledge to analyse the security camera system, looking for flaws in it. Spend several days on this to ensure you understand the complete system. We will then talk again in about a week to hear your findings."

Next, he called forward Jonathan, his son, Michael, also George and Peter. He addressed all four together with the same instructions. "You will all be given covert cameras disguised as pocket pens or buttons. You will visit the casino each day and play blackjack using all the tricks and techniques you have been taught. You will be given 10,000 Quetzals; about £1,000 each day to play skilfully with. Every evening when you return to Pathways, we will cash in your daily result and record it. After Kokee and I have analysed your body cameras to see what worked, what didn't and why, we will then go through the results after dinner each day. This way, we can all learn and improve your play."

This left two recruits without roles. They were Angela and Matt. Antonio spoke to them both next. He explained that their initial roles were to essentially be as observers, also with body cameras. They could play the roulette table, only with very small bets. They would be given just 1,000 Quetzals each and, whilst not really expected to win, they had to make the money last for as long as possible. Their hidden cameras were not so much to record games but to observe other people.

Now, he was interrupted with questions. Peter spoke first. "I am not any kind of elected spokesperson for us, but do speak on behalf of most of us when I say we are becoming increasingly concerned about this whole scheme. Is what we are being asked to do legal and what happens if we are questioned by the casino owners? Finally, how long is this going to continue and, most importantly, when can we be released with our passports, which is what I believe we all want?"

Antonio did his best to reassure them all and promised that this mission wouldn't take much longer and committed that they soon would be free to leave, complete with their passports. He also assured them they could not possibly face any legal consequences for this work.

They seemed to accept this response, albeit a little reluctantly.

"Now," he said. "Kokee is going to give you a little history of our currency that you may find interesting or perhaps useful."

She then explained the origin of the 'Quetzal'.

"The Quetzal was introduced here in 1925 during the term of President Jose Maria Orellana, whose image still appears to this day on the reverse side of the one-quetzal bill. It replaced our peso at the rate of sixty to one. Little known is that, until 1987, the Quetzal was pegged to and equal to the United States dollar!"

As she continued, all seemed most interested in this history, some even made copious notes on what they were hearing.

"The name of this currency came from our national bird, the quetzal. In ancient Mayan culture, this bird's tail feathers were actually used as money. Today, there are about ten quetzals to your UK pound."

With that, she sat down. The history lesson for the day was over.

Those who needed covert cameras were given them, along with instructions to ensure they were switched on whenever they were inside the casino and to diligently charge them in their rooms every night after the footage had been downloaded to the Pathways' computer.

With that done and money handed out as agreed, they were all given their rotas so each knew when to go to the casino and for how long. These rotas gave them each four days to do their tasks and three free days to do as they wished. All then set off to the casino to begin their work.

Chapter 19

Back in Chester, England, Maria was far from giving up her mission of finding her estranged husband who had run off with a substantial lottery win. Maria knew that legally she was entitled to half and she was determined to get it.

The police had been as helpful as they could, placing him on that San Francisco flight but, as he had committed no criminal offence, they were not interested in the civil matter that was clearly now the case.

She then enlisted the services of a private investigator who came up with a proposition that suited her.

Whilst she had little money and couldn't afford the kind of fees normally charged by this profession, a positive outcome of locating his whereabouts would change that quite quickly. Realising this, Michael Strattan, the private investigator, proposed a commission on results, otherwise no fee was to be charged. He explained that his required rate would be ten per cent of her share. She readily agreed and signed his contract.

The police had already confirmed that, whilst George certainly boarded the British Airways flight at London airport, he did not board it again on its unscheduled second leg from Pinal Airfield.

Michael booked a one-way flight to Phoenix, Arizona. As he had no way of knowing how long he would be away, he packed a bag with enough clothes to last several weeks. His flight was for the following Tuesday. It was an American Airlines flight, number AA195, departing at 9.45 am from Heathrow. The scheduled flight time was eleven hours.

He arrived at the airport by taxi, trying to avoid very expensive airport long-term parking fees. He checked in and was pleased that the flight was quickly ready for boarding and subsequently departed on time.

He slept for much of what was a comfortable and uneventful flight.

On arrival in Phoenix, he checked into a budget motel. From there, he booked a day return sightseeing trip to Pinal Airfield not far away. There, he took the regular tour around all the planes and, showing a great interest in all the aircraft, he succeeded in establishing a very good relationship with the airport manager, Jim Petty.

He had a list of questions about the airfield and the managing of it. These were to be addressed to Jim after the tour. What Michael really wanted to know, of course, was what happened to those passengers who never took the onward flight to San Francisco.

He asked Jim if he could interview him for an article he claimed to be writing about the airfield. Jim agreed and invited him into his office for coffee.

Skilfully, he steered the conversation towards the mystery of some people who disappeared from an emergency flight that had arrived from London several weeks before. He explained that this had aroused public interest in the UK and that solving this would further enhance his article about the airfield and the skilled management of it by its manager.

Flattered, Jim explained that only one other flight had departed the airfield that day and confirmed that it was a small private charter plane cleared to Guatemala City Airport. This was all Michael wanted to know, but to disguise this, he asked further questions about Jim's work and his background. He even went as far as to take photographs of him for 'his article'.

He returned to his hotel in Phoenix on the return seat he had already booked for that same evening.

He now knew where his next stop was going to be. He arrived at the motel late in the evening and, being tired, went straight to bed. He felt he had done a good day's work and was making progress. He decided to update Maria the following afternoon by phone, taking into account the eight-hour time difference with the UK.

The following afternoon, Michael booked a one-way flight to Guatemala City Airport for late the next morning. He settled back into his motel room to rest as jet lag had now caught up with him a little.

He later took a taxi into town and went to a bank to change some UK pounds into the local Guatemalan currency in readiness for the time he knew he would need to spend there.

He found an Indian restaurant he liked the look of. Indian food had become one of his favourites over the years. Gradually, as his taste buds became accustomed to the spices the Indians used so liberally, he then ordered his dishes as 'hot' rather than the mild or medium he had taken before! He chose an onion bhaji to start, followed by a lamb jalfrezi with pilau rice, a Peshawari nan, and a side of saag aloo. He washed it all down with a couple of Cobra Indian beers.

On returning to his motel, he quickly fell into a rather heavy sleep. His snoring could probably be heard by anyone in an adjoining room.

Early the following morning, he checked out of this little motel and took a taxi to the airport in good time for his 11.45 flight to Guatemala City Airport.

It wasn't long before his flight was called for boarding. After boarding, the flight took off on time with no fuss. The plane was barely fifty per cent full, so he had empty seats on either side of him.

This flight to Guatemala took almost seven hours. On arriving at this airport, he set his watch ahead one hour to seven-thirty in the evening. On leaving the small terminal, he asked his taxi driver to recommend a mid-priced nearby hotel and take him there. After a short drive, he arrived at the La Inmaculada, a three-star hotel. He checked in and went to his room. It was spacious and comfortable.

Having eaten at both Phoenix Airport and again on the flight, he had no further need to leave his room that evening. He sat down with his file on this missing person and made some notes and plans for the days ahead. He realised that finding this man, even if this was his final destination, would be something of a challenge, to say the least.

All these travelling and time zone changes were taking their toll on Michael, so again he slept very soundly.

He was awakened at 3 am by several police sirens screaming in the street outside his window, one he had left open for some cooler air overnight. It took him quite a while to get back to sleep. He eventually surfaced at 8 am and went down to breakfast. This was a typical cold buffet selection which was fine for his needs today. Michael found out later that there had been a fight in the town in the early hours resulting in a serious stabbing of a youth.

Taking several copies of recent photos of his prey with him, a certain George Middleton, he set off on foot into the town.

His first port of call was a large central taxi rank; here there was a line of about a dozen taxis. He systematically showed each driver a picture of George along with a pre-translated sheet of paper all in Spanish. In essence, it read: *Have you seen this man? I am offering a reward for information as to his whereabouts.* This first part of Michael's search yielded no result of any kind.

That first day, he made similar enquiries at the bus station booking office and also at the small train station. Everything so far drew a blank.

He wasn't surprised or discouraged, he knew this would take time. He was tenacious and, having come this far, was determined to get his man!

After stopping for a small late tapas lunch at 3 pm, he returned to his hotel room. Here, he updated Maria on the progress so far by email. Due to the various time differences, they were experiencing and also the considerable phone costs involved with communications, it had now been agreed this would be their means of future progress updates.

After a short siesta, he settled down to watch a film on the room's TV. It was an old Western. The speech was all in Spanish but it had subtitles in English, so he could easily follow this film; it was actually one he had seen several years before.

The following morning, he again went into town to further his quest to locate George Middleton. He felt he had come a long way and was close, however, he knew that the last steps were often the most difficult.

He went around all the central cafés, bars, and restaurants. Each time showing George's picture but each time receiving a negative response.

He stopped for a brief lunch at a charming little restaurant, teasingly called 'The Best'. He had to admit later that it was very good, although having had little chance to try all the others, he couldn't say whether their name was completely accurate for certain!

After paying a very reasonable bill, less than half of that he would have paid back home, he left to continue his search. His next port of call was now the local police station. Here, he was surprised at how friendly they were, having been used to the all too often abrupt attitude of those in the UK.

Despite this, after careful inspection of the photo, the sergeant at the reception desk informed him that he had no recollection of ever seeing this person in the local area.

Then, just as Michael was about to leave, a plainclothes officer came in. He enquired of the desk officer what the problem was. A short chat ensued between them in Spanish. Too fast for Michael to understand. This newcomer asked to also see a copy of the photo. Michael gladly showed it to him, keen to obtain all the help he could get, however small. After studying the picture carefully, his facial expression gave hope…it showed a possible recognition perhaps?

He asked Michael to wait for a few minutes whilst he went to check some records he had in his office. Wow, Michael could hardly contain his excitement. Was he onto inside? Was he onto George at last?

After what seemed an eternity; although in reality was just twenty minutes, he returned to deliver the best news Michael could possibly have hoped for.

He informed him that he had seen this individual on several occasions in the town centre casino, gambling at the tables.

He went on to explain that they were investigating this casino undercover and had covert video of many punters there. George, though of no interest to them, was present in several of these videos. It was those that he had gone back to his office computer to view.

After obtaining directions to the casino and thanking the Guatemalan police profoundly, he set off again. After a short walk, he located the brightly lit casino and ventured inside. This was an establishment of a kind he had never been in before. He was amazed at the size, the bright lights, and the incessant noise that filled his head. Noticing the many security cameras everywhere, Michael decided that he couldn't just hang around without seeming to have a purpose, so he purchased a small quantity of low-value chips and also some small coins that would be accepted by the electronic gambling machines. 'Fruit machines' as he knew them as a youngster, wasting his money and time on them in his then local pub!

After spending about the equivalent of some £200, as slowly as he could, he left about three hours later. He noticed girls giving free drinks to those gamblers on the higher-value tables; they offered him none!

He had quite enjoyed his time spent there but had not developed a taste for gambling. It seemed that the odds were not in the favour of the punter. Especially one as inexperienced as he.

Realising that George would be unlikely to play there every day, he knew that return visits and patience were surely required for the coming days.

Back in his hotel room, he sent a message to George's wife, Maria, informing her of his progress that day. He assured her that he was certain he was very close now. The day had been tiring and, in fact, the excitement of this latest development had taken up quite a bit of his natural resources. So, after a small in-room dinner service of ham and chips, he went to his bed, again exhausted.

The following morning, he was up early, keen to get back to the casino by 10 am when they opened.

Despite spending several more hours there and, more importantly, losing another lump of his travel money (this visit it was just over £300), he kept reminding himself that ten per cent of her share of some £3 million would handsomely cover all these unexpected costs.

It was on his fourth day spent losing money that his luck changed. He spotted George at a blackjack table. He just observed him for a while and couldn't help noticing that he seemed to win fairly consistently. George clearly was more experienced than him.

After a short while, he managed to strike up a brief conversation with him. George was willing to chat with this new acquaintance, particularly as he missed talking to someone who spoke full English.

Michael ascertained that he was living in a local hotel having left the UK to get a divorce. After only a few minutes of chatting, Michael showed his hand. He told George that he was a private detective and it had been his mission this time to track him down. It was now clear to George that the game was up, he had been found and was just about to be exposed. He realised that he couldn't now just run away. He would be followed from now onwards and besides, he was all too well aware that he held no passport.

George was clear in his mind immediately that, whilst he was willing to square up his financial debt with his wife, he didn't want to see her again. He also made up his mind that he would do nothing to expose his fellow inmates, several of whom had become real friends after so much time working and living together.

There was no animosity between them. George had secretly been regretting what he had done. He had no desire to continue a life with Maria but was starting to think that he had been rather unfair to her. At the end of the day, several million was a lot of money, whether it be six or three. He knew that any amount would give him a very comfortable lifestyle for the remainder of his days.

Michael was also clearly a decent guy, just doing a job. He made it clear that he had no desire to expose George or his exact location. He just was seeking a fair financial settlement for Maria. They agreed to adjourn to a local restaurant to negotiate terms that could be acceptable to all. They went to 'The Best' restaurant where Michael was immediately recognised and greeted like a long-lost brother.

George had one more dishonest card to play, however. He convinced Michael that since leaving the UK, he had not only cleared several substantial (fictitious) debts he and Maria had, but he had lost much of the winnings. He told Michael he only had about £5 million left. Despite the fact that he had only spent about £39,000 and change, he still had the full £6 million. Michael believed him and suggested a settlement of £2.5 million.

George realised he was not in a strong position and, on a few conditions, agreed there and then to this settlement. His terms were simple. He would transfer this sum to her bank through a numbered offshore account within seven days.

The conditions were;

1. His location and new name would remain confidential and never be disclosed.
2. She would accept a divorce.
3. She would agree, in writing, that this was a full and final settlement.
4. Michael would make no attempt to contact him or his friends there ever again.
5. He would sign over ownership of their house to her one hundred per cent.

Michael wrote down these terms carefully and they decided to meet the following day again, same place, same time. They went their separate ways after George was left to pay for the refreshments they had consumed. This deal seemed to be acceptable to these two men, but it yet had to be agreed with the 'boss'. During the following few days, it was finally all legally agreed. George made the transfer and got back on with his new life.

We will never know how Maria really felt, but it surely would have been hard to be unhappy after just receiving £2.5 million, as well as a house in addition.

Chapter 20

The Pathways team was busy each week making frequent visits with some winning money and all were also learning valuable information every visit.

Antonio and Kokee had a brief meeting with all who had been in the casino every day. Money was counted, taken, and recorded as needed. More importantly, covert body camera footage was downloaded to their mainframe business computer for careful inspection.

Much was learnt in these first weeks and after eight weeks, some 200,000 Quetzals had been won. This was about £20,000. It was a good start but a drop in the ocean of what was needed. After a detailed meeting with each, Antonio made a new plan for some of them.

The main one was based on information from Wan. He was quite an electronics expert it had turned out. He explained to Antonio that their security system was archaic, he particularly referred to the camera surveillance setup. Antonio didn't understand the technicalities of the information Wan was imparting but got the gist of it. The system was out-of-date, unreliable, and quite easy to defraud.

He asked Wan to obtain an appointment with whoever was the most senior of the current owners and attempt to get a job to help them by substantially upgrading their system and thereby increasing their vital security. This took rather longer than expected as the remaining two criminals running the casino were very canny. They viewed everyone with suspicion, Wan was included.

After a couple of weeks, he had the little piece of luck he needed. He noticed that one of the cameras had a blinking red LED on the front that had recently appeared. He pointed this out to Rafael, one of the new owners, and offered to give the system a complete overhaul and upgrade. He offered his services for a quite ridiculously low price to secure the job. His offer was accepted.

After reporting this exciting new development to Antonio and Kokee, he was given the funds he needed to purchase the required tools to convince Rafael that he was genuine in his work. More importantly, he would be able to make changes to the camera system, changes that would give Pathways the next move they needed.

The next part of the plan was down to the lovely Joanna. Her job was to obtain a significant promotion in the casino. Antonio needed her to become a croupier at a blackjack table and to end her waitress work. To do this, she needed to reuse her past work experience, that of a hooker.

Over a remarkably short time, she managed to succesfully get into Rafael's bed.

This was done reluctantly as she had developed a close and affectionate relationship with Jonathan's son, Michael, and found this rather sordid because of that. She knew, however, that she had a job to do; this was just a part of it.

Once she was giving Rafael the sex he craved, she didn't have to wait long before he trusted her enough to let her loose as a croupier on one of the blackjack tables.

There were security cameras everywhere and the most important ones were over these gambling tables. Every move made by the croupier and punters alike was monitored live and also recorded. Wan's job was to modify the actions of the camera over her table. When punters want to buy chips, with cash, it can occur at the table with the chips being given out by the croupier.

In doing so, the dealer is required to hold up the payment method for the camera to see and, for example, has to say clearly 'changing one thousand'. The camera records everything, especially the value of the chips being passed across the table. This should make it impossible for any fraud.

Assuming the camera is on!

Wan's job was to find a way to disable Joanna's table camera for three minutes each day in such a way that the resulting footage would appear seamless. This, he managed to do. It was set for precisely 2 pm every Wednesday. Only he, Joanna, and Peter knew.

Peter's job was to be on her table and to change up money for chips at exactly the right time the following Wednesday. It went like clockwork. He changed up about £4,000 and, whilst the camera was having a siesta, discretely received ten times as many chips.

Over the following weeks, this illusion took place smoothly on several occasions. The casino was now beginning to haemorrhage significant money without a trace.

Things were going well for Antonio and Kokee at the moment. But was this to last?

Chapter 21

As the days and weeks passed by, all seemed to be progressing slowly but successfully for Antonio.

The guests were finding their feet in their new environment. They were meeting people in the town, enjoying the weather and their freedom.

One of the things they marvelled at was the little tuk-tuks that raced around everywhere, crazily darting in and out of the other traffic. They all started to use them as very cheap taxis.

Matt was far from content with his situation, however. He had two passions; firstly, a love of flying, and secondly, rather darkly, a craving for young teenage girls, those preferably less than sixteen. He knew he couldn't, nor never would, fulfil either of these needs at Pathways. He, therefore, decided to seek a way out.

He began to look for two things—possible work and also accommodation. It didn't take him long to locate a small local airfield that offered flying lessons. They used the very same small single prop planes he had originally learnt on.

He met with the manager of the airfield and it didn't take long for him to secure a part-time instructor job teaching people to fly. His past experience, all the way up to 'Jumbo' jets enrolled him instantly.

Now, he needed accommodation. This proved more difficult as demand exceeded the availability of budget-priced apartments.

He quickly realised that to secure one, he would have to pay top dollar. This he reluctantly agreed to do and took possession a few days later. He had, of course, got the main day-to-day documents, a bank account, and a mobile phone all in his new name, but what he didn't have was a passport—Antonio had that—and there was no way to get it for the moment. That would be a step for him later.

At Pathways, Antonio and the rest of the team realised that Matt had left but they were not deterred from continuing their work with the final goal of a full passport freedom.

Angela was basically ok, but as a lesbian, was missing a partner; she still hadn't fully got over the split with her past lover.

In her visits to the town, she was always on the lookout for someone. She eventually found a gay nightclub on the east side of the town. It was a bit what you would describe as seedy, but she felt it could perhaps serve a purpose. She joined as a member. This move turned out to be a disastrous decision for just about everyone.

One Thursday night in March, she struck up a conversation with an attractive girl from Barcelona, Spain mainland. Her name was Lucia. Angela was immediately attracted to her, also she to Angela. They just talked and drank that evening but agreed to meet again the following week.

Angela could think of little else each of the following nights lying alone naked in her bed. She was hungry and it wasn't for food.

Kokee was in great spirits and was planning a special celebration for Antonio's upcoming fortieth birthday on the 17th of April. Antonio's father had told him that, contrary to the norm, it had rained heavily on that day. April was typically about the warmest month of the year in Guatemala with most afternoon temperatures at around 27 degrees. Rainfall was also very rare in that month.

Statistics for past years showed just two wet days in the month. His father told him that he remembered getting absolutely drenched running from his parked car to the maternity ward at their local hospital. Most unlucky on that day clearly.

Kokee had arranged a marquee in their extensive grounds for this special birthday celebration; it was to be set close to the huge swimming pool the hotel had.

She invited many friends and dignitaries. These included the local mayor, Carlos Armas. He had served the local community for the past eleven years and was very popular. A recent move he made won the overwhelming support of the local residents when he banned electric scooters from their streets. They had experienced awful incidents of children, as young as ten, riding two at a time on pavements and one-way streets the wrong way on frequent occasions. When it resulted in the death of an innocent man in his seventies, they all agreed enough was enough. So, he was more than popular, even though most considered him to be gay, still living with his mother at fifty-seven years of age.

Another celebrity invited was Marvin Ramirez, the top basketball player from two years before. He was a local resident and had often frequented

Antonio's restaurant with his lovely, six-foot model wife, Ana. All was getting set for an extravaganza of a day.

Angela and Lucia took their lesbian relationship all the way. When I say, all the way, I mean sexually. As it turned out later, there was no love between them.

There was quite an argument when the company came to erect the marquee for Antonio's big day. It turned out that the one the trailer had delivered was not the one she had ordered. She had specified particular colours and lovely blue inside lights. This one they had brought fulfilled neither of these needs. It was swiftly dismissed back to where it had come from. Nobody messed with Kokee!

This was just the start. Many meetings, discussions, and changes took place in the following days. Including the hiring of a security company whose job would be to ensure nobody 'gate-crashed' the party without an invite.

Angela's relationship continued with Lucia, but it was not all as it had first appeared. What Angela didn't know was that she was Rafael's sister, a co-owner of the casino. Angela's pillow talk slowly informed Lucia of the Pathways' scheme.

Chapter 22

By now, with the exception of Matt, everyone else had now settled into their routines at Pathways, their casino visits, and time spent around the town on their free days.

Peter discovered a lovely piano bar where, with his passion for music, he spent many of his free evenings. Here, he became fascinated by a local instrument known as the Marimba that was often featured there. It was something like a xylophone but with wooden keys and long hanging wooden tubes. He learnt that the longer the plate, the lower the note it produced. Later, he looked into the possibility of purchasing one but was shocked to find how expensive they were. Best quality ones ran into thousands of UK pounds! There were cheap copies available, but the sounds they produced were not anywhere near the quality Peter wanted. He decided not to purchase one until the day came that he could afford the real thing.

Wan hired a small car one afternoon to explore further afield. He had located a car dealership in the area that usually had a few cars available, but no sign of the Ferrari he really wanted.

On discussion with the owner, it transpired that he could generally source any vehicle that was being sought by a prospective buyer. Wan promptly set him the task of finding a particular model he wanted, the 296 GTB Roma. Depending upon the exact model and specification, it transpired that the price for a new one would be in the region of £300,000. Wan could obviously afford that, but being shrewd with his money, he set the dealer on the mission of finding a low-mileage model of around five years of age. He specified that it had to be red.

He then set off in his small hire car to try out the area's roads to test their suitability for stretching a Ferrari's legs, should he be fortunate enough to be able to purchase one.

George decided that he might try his hand at golf. Other than a bit of 'Pitch & Putt' as a youngster, he had never even been on a golf course, let alone swung a real club. Antonio told him where the local course was and gave him directions. He visited on one of his free afternoons and took a look.

He was warmly welcomed by Pablo, the course manager. George explained that he was a novice and looking to try golf out with a view to taking a course of lessons. Pablo gave him a quotation for five thirty-minute sessions with an instructor to be used over a four-week period.

The quoted price of 2,500 Quetzals included the hire of a half set of clubs; enough to begin with he was told. George calculated this at about £50 a session. He thought it most reasonable. He later found out that such a package would easily cost twice as much in the USA, probably even more in Europe. He paid his subscription and booked his first session for the following Friday. It was explained to him what shoes and clothing would be appropriate. He realised that the special shoes at least would need to be purchased, so he was glad to have a week's notice before this first lesson.

Before leaving, he had a look around the club and its facilities. He also took in a glass of beer in the clubhouse, which was very elegant and spacious. It was aptly named 'Hole 19'. Then, it was back to Pathways to continue his work for Antonio and Kokee.

Jonathan and his son, Michael, had joined a local snooker club where they spent many enjoyable evenings playing. Usually with each other, but occasionally taking on locals in doubles matches. Michael often got angry with his father when he made poor shots, which he did often, resulting in them losing games and often small wagers.

When playing each other, Jonathan got frustrated because he had to reluctantly accept that his son was the better player. This was due to three reasons: more recent practice, his superior height and hence his reach for long shots, and finally, just his youthful untrammelled eyesight. Nevertheless, with little else to do in their evenings, these games were still just about worthwhile and enjoyable.

When Michael wasn't with his father, he was spending an increasing amount of time with Joanna. She had by this time cooled off and ended her 'relationship' with Rafael, having achieved the goal set for her by Antonio, namely that of becoming a croupier at one of the casino's tables.

So, that was the state of play at Pathways. Matt having departed, left the remaining seven inmates getting on with their tasks and lives with a kind of freedom. Certainly better than they each would have experienced had they remained in the UK much longer.

Chapter 23

Whilst preparations for Antonio's fortieth birthday party were busily underway, Rafael and Sergio were also making plans for that day, but theirs were not the kind that would be welcomed by anyone else. They had discovered Antonio's plans and were set on a path of revenge; one that they intended would put an end to his permanently.

The 3rd of April came, a special day in Guatemala. Not a happy day but one of remembrance.

Seven years before, a powerful earthquake struck the city at 2.36 in the morning. It registered 8.3 on the Richter Scale and caused extensive damage. Some buildings, the more poorly constructed ones, collapsed completely. Most people were asleep in their beds and were caught up in it with little or no warning. It lasted a mere three minutes but was frightening. One hundred and twelve citizens perished that night, fifteen of them were children and scores of others were injured, many seriously. One miracle happened when about eighteen hours later, a baby was pulled out of the rubble still alive and with little injury. She was still in the crib that had saved her due to its particularly sturdy construction.

Every year on this date, a two-minute silence was held at midday to remember this tragic event and those who died. This year, the atmosphere was not improved by a heavy rainstorm on that day, rather uncharacteristic for the time of year. Some felt it was a sign from above.

Kokee's sister was one of the unfortunate who died in her bed that fateful night. Like in previous years, Kokee and Antonio together visited their small cemetery and laid flowers during the two minutes of silence and reflection. A sad day which could only offer the positive of a few hours when their minds were not on their other problems.

The following day, Kokee set her mind back to getting on with Antonio's birthday preparations. She had just two weeks to go and still much left to do. The initial list of guests invited totalled one hundred and sixteen adults and eighteen children. All had now replied and just seven of them declined the invitation due to other unavoidable commitments, so seating, food, and refreshments for a hundred and twenty-seven guests were arranged. The cost was already exceeding the budget Kokee had planned on but she kept the total sum from Antonio so as to not cast any shadow on what was planned to be a lovely day.

Antonio had spent some time talking to his brother during the days before the party, having not seen him for so long. His brother had seemed somewhat distant on arrival and Antonio was trying to ascertain why. It quickly became apparent that Carlos was unhappy at not having been picked as Antonio's best man for his wedding and that he resented having to pick up the pieces of the coffee plantation business on his own. In addition, he seemed somewhat jealous of his brother's achievements and the happy marriage he clearly had. They talked several times over the few days before the party but it was never warm; it never felt right.

After a very busy few days, the preparations were complete; every last detail was taken care of. Little did anyone suspect what the remaining two casino managers had in store for the day.

It finally came, the 17th of April, Antonio's big day!

The caterers arrived on time at 10 am and began to lay out the tables to Kokee's clear and specific written instructions. The weather was lovely with clear skies and a pleasant temperature. This was in line with the forecast of 27 degrees mid-afternoon with, fortunately, no sign of the rain that had occurred on the day he had been born.

There was a long top table to seat a select number of VIPs. Kokee and Antonio were in the centre of this, with Antonio's brother on one side of them and the mayor and his mother on the other. Also, on this top table was Marvin Ramirez, the famous basketball player, along with his wife and their son as well.

The guests started to arrive at 2 pm as planned. By 2.45, all had arrived and settled in to enjoy a day that had started with champagne; Spanish cava, of course!

The conversations were lively and jovial. Whilst many knew each other, there were still plenty of introductions to be made for first meetings. Many took this opportunity to make new friends.

The meal was served at precisely 3 pm, exactly as per Kokee's instructions. All was going to plan so far.

A few weeks earlier, Rafael and Sergio, the casino managers and part owners had fully formulated their revenge attack on Antonio. They obtained a rifle online that had been advertised by a North American dealer. It was a budget-priced H & R 280 single shot Remmington. It cost $270. No ammunition was included as shipping this required one of the most difficult to obtain licences. They, however, quite easily were able to purchase a box of twenty rounds at a local dealer. This was far more than they expected to use. They hoped that just one shot would be enough.

Chapter 24

When the guests had finished their meal, a couple of speeches followed.

Kokee stood up first and, as is traditional on these occasions, tapped a glass to obtain everyone's attention.

"Firstly, thank you all for coming to help celebrate my husband's fortieth birthday this afternoon. We would especially like to welcome some VIPs, namely our mayor, Carlos Armas, and his mother, also our greatest ever basketball player, Marvin Ramirez, and his charming wife." There was then a spontaneous round of applause for these dignitaries.

With that, Kokee proposed the first of several toasts to her husband, who beamed from ear to ear. She sat back down and then Antonio took to his feet.

Rafael and Sergio were on a small ridge some fifty metres from the entrance to the hotel grounds, where two security guards were on duty. This was the moment they had been patiently waiting for. The rifle was loaded, cocked, and ready to do its evil work. Both were apprehensive as to whether they could pull this off. They were sweating profusely.

The hundred and twenty-seven guests all fell silent in anticipation. They made a spectacle, all dressed in their finery. Kokee had specified a particular tasteful dress code for the day, not too formal but nevertheless very smart. Long trousers and closed shoes were stipulated for the men, for example.

At this point, the hired photographer recorded the entire group from every angle. Kokee wanted lovely memories of this day.

A loud crack was suddenly heard and Kokee slumped to the floor. Most had no idea what the sound was. Some thought it a car backfiring, others thought of a firework perhaps. Those at the front, seeing Kokee crash to the floor, were in no illusions; they realised immediately that she had been shot. Screams were heard and panic was suddenly everywhere.

Antonio and others at the top table went to Kokee's aid. Her dress was red in the middle, clearly from blood. She was bleeding from her abdomen. Someone pulled the dress away from the affected area and applied a wad of the linen tablecloth in an attempt to stem the bleeding.

"Call for an ambulance and a doctor!" Antonio screamed at the top of his voice.

Just eighteen minutes later, this vital assistance arrived and Kokee was put on a stretcher and rapidly, but carefully, put into the waiting ambulance. Antonio went in too, never letting go of her hand. It sped away, siren blaring, heading directly to the local hospital just a few minutes away. Inside the speeding ambulance, two medics were in attendance. One had noticed she was delirious, just 'out of it', not knowing where she was. Antonio could also see she was finding breathing difficult and becoming unconscious. Swiftly, she was put on oxygen and the wound's bleeding was properly halted.

Back in the hotel grounds, the police had also arrived. There were two of them. They appealed for calm and asked everyone to remain in their seats. They would all need to be interviewed to ascertain what had happened, what they saw and what assistance they could offer in the investigation. An investigation that was going to be clearly one of attempted murder at the very least.

The ambulance arrived quickly at the accident and emergency entrance of the Hospital Santa Margarita. It wasn't quickly as far as Antonio felt as he described later. It had felt like an age.

His wife, his soul mate and best friend, was seriously injured, perhaps fatally.

Antonio was guided to a visitors' room and given a questionnaire to complete about Kokee.

After somehow completing the necessary form with a shaking pen, it was collected by one of the staff, who assured him that his wife was in the best possible hands and that a doctor would update him the very moment there was some news. At first, he paced up and down, refusing to sit or take any of the refreshments a nurse offered him. Eventually, he did sit down, crying with his head in his hands, in deep despair. *Why? Who?* It was making no sense to him.

The police were meanwhile taking statements from those who could offer any information. Most could add little to what had become obvious that Kokee had been shot by someone outside the hotel grounds. Two people sat at the back were, however, able to offer some information that later would become vital in solving this terrible crime.

They had both realised where the crack had come from and turned to look in that approximate direction. They both agreed that two men, dressed in dark clothes, ran towards a small white car and then raced away tyres screeching. Whilst they couldn't identify the car in any way, other than to say it was white, there was however a piece of important information they were able to give.

They said that the car had an unusual and very loud exhaust sound, most likely caused by a defective silencer they suggested.

Antonio now had been joined by two of his hotel staff, both of which were very close friends. They were Pablo and Isabel.

It seemed like hours, but was, in reality, less than one, before a doctor came out to speak to Antonio. In an effort to calm him, he first assured Antonio that she was stable and expected to make a full recovery after surgery; however, there was more information to impart. He said, "Antonio, may I call you that?" Antonio promptly responded in the affirmative. He went on, "Kokee is still unconscious, but whilst breathing fairly normally, she is on a low dose of oxygen as a precaution. She is in shock as would be expected. When that happens, the brain shuts the body down to allow it to pick back up. This is normal considering what she has experienced."

"We have taken several x-rays of her lower abdomen, where the bullet entered. We have learnt three things. Firstly, no vital organs were affected and she is not bleeding internally, or even externally now. Secondly, the bullet entered but made no exit. It is wedged into her lower spine. This can be removed and indeed should be; more on that in a minute. Lastly, did you know that your wife was pregnant?"

This last part was a bombshell to Antonio. He stuttered, "No, I had no idea of this."

The doctor continued. "First, we have to allow her to come around naturally, which she will shortly; we are sure of this. Then, we will need to discuss the next treatment. This is something both of you will need to discuss and agree to. Let me explain what is the hard truth and the difficult decision to be made. One which the two of you alone can make."

Antonio was trembling at this point, realising there was something coming that was not going to make good listening. "If we undertake surgery to remove the bullet, which is our medical recommendation, you will likely lose the baby. We may need to abort the foetus in order to safely perform the very delicate procedure of removing the bullet. If we don't remove this bullet, you will probably save the pregnancy but Kokee will almost certainly be paralysed, in constant pain, and on medication for the rest of her life. So, it will boil down to a choice of Kokee's future well-being or that of your unborn child, which is a boy incidentally."

This was just too much for Antonio to take in. He dropped his head into his hands and sobbed uncontrollably. A nurse quickly came to his side in an attempt to comfort him. A relaxant was proposed and subsequently taken. He asked if he could see Kokee and was told he could come through and sit at her bedside for as long as he wanted. He duly followed the doctor, as did his two friends, anxious to support him at this harrowing time.

They were taken to a neat but small private room and offered refreshments; his friends declined but Antonio requested a cup of tea.

They sat at the bedside, watching her sleep peacefully. He held her hand. It was warm. He wasn't sure whether the clammy feel was caused by her or by him.

No one spoke; they just held vigil and probably prayed. There was nothing else they could do at the moment, except to again think…Who? Why?

What would they decide to do?

Chapter 25

The police were all over this case; nothing like this had happened before in such a quiet neighbourhood. They didn't allow anyone to leave the hotel until they had sufficient statements to compile a complete picture.

Another piece of information emerged that was most interesting. Namely, the shot had been made as soon as Antonio took to his feet, but not before Kokee had leant across him to reposition the microphone in an effort to assist his planned speech. It was looking increasingly as though the bullet may have been intended for Antonio; Kokee may have just got in the way at the wrong moment. One of the guests had been making a video of the proceedings and gave a copy of it to the police.

Now, the main mission for them was to speak with Antonio to try to ascertain what enemy or enemies he had that could have been behind this terrible crime.

They subsequently visited him at the hospital and tactfully asked him if he would be willing to leave Kokee's bedside for a few minutes to talk to them. They stressed that they needed this discussion to assist their enquiries into the case and to eventually bring whoever was guilty to justice. Realising that time was of the essence, he duly agreed to their request straight away.

Antonio was not only still in shock, but also affected by the sedative he had just been given, and therefore was of little help to the police during this initial interview. He returned to Kokee's bedside where he remained for the evening and a very long sleepless night.

Back at Pathways, his remaining seven recruits, having been fully briefed on what had occurred, jointly agreed to take a break and cease their 'operations' at the casino until further instructions. Whilst all had concern for Kokee and indeed Antonio, they welcomed the break to have some quality time to themselves.

Peter was beginning to think this could be the end of their mission and that he may be able to obtain possession of his new passport and therefore his freedom. He had missed the UK, not enjoying the lifestyle in Guatemala at all.

He decided that, given the chance, he would return to the UK with his new identity. He was confident he could find a good management position in another company, even though no reference or CV would be possible. At this point, he had little thought for anyone but himself.

Joanna knew she couldn't again make herself a model in the public eye for fear of being recognised as Joanna Crawly rather than Joanna Devine, as she now was. So whilst she wanted to leave, she yet didn't know what career she could safely pursue. She too was focused on only herself.

Wan, in contrast, was actually very content living there but was most concerned for Kokee's welfare at this moment and eagerly awaiting Antonio's return with news. Wan was, of course, also looking forward to the delivery of the Ferrari he had ordered. He had finally decided on a new one; a decent second-hand one seeming impossible to find. This way, he was getting a detailed specification exactly to his choice. Red, of course! If released from this hotel, he had already earmarked an area he liked that had nice properties for sale. He would wait patiently for his masters to return and divulge their plans, hopefully new ones.

Jonathan's son, Michael, now had a deep relationship with Joanna and indeed had by now moved into her room. They discussed what options they had. She was an attractive model, with a job at the casino; he was a qualified mechanic, something in short supply locally. So, they clearly both had options.

His father, Jonathan, as a retired well-built boxer, had already been offered work in a security capacity at the snooker club he had joined. The need for this position was accelerated by some recent violence by teenage youths fighting over a game. All over whether a shot on the black was a foul or not! Jonathan willingly stepped in and sorted these reprobates out. Even three were no match for him!

The management made him a temporary job offer on the spot. They both clearly had things to consider.

Angela was missing her birthplace of Scotland. Despite the often brutal weather, she loved it. She had no family there, so knew she could return to a different part without being identified as a McHaig. She was now a MacDonald. Along with the others, she also pondered Antonio's future plans and what her own would be in response.

George was perhaps the most content of them all. He had his golf club membership and played as often as he could. He had become addicted, as so many seem to, and was improving rapidly. He told everyone that he wished he had discovered this hobby so much earlier.

He also had plenty of money and nothing really to spend it on. What he lacked was just his new passport to give him complete independence. It was fair to say, however, that he had become attached to both Kokee and Antonio and was very comfortable at Pathways. He just was looking forward to ending their 'work' at the casino. That, he didn't enjoy at all.

Now, Matt was a very different story. He had left, without warning or a passport. He didn't seem to care. He had his own place and a decent job, teaching pupils to fly planes. That would perhaps have been fine had he truly put his past behind him. This was something that wasn't going to prove quite so easy.

Chapter 26

After several long days and nights had passed, Kokee suddenly opened her eyes one morning at about 6 am. Antonio was half in and half out of sleep but instinctively became alert. "Where am I?" She asked in a slightly slurred voice that didn't sound anything like her.

"You are in the hospital and I am with you." She seemed puzzled and was clearly not yet fully awake. Antonio swiftly alerted the day nurse by pressing the button beside the bed provided for this very eventuality. Within seconds, a staff nurse arrived followed a few moments later by her doctor.

They took her pulse and checked her blood pressure. Under the circumstances, the doctor confirmed all was well.

Antonio slowly and purposefully explained to her what had happened. He assured her she was going to fully recover in a short while and that she should try to rest and just follow the doctor's advice for now. He, however, omitted to mention anything about the pregnancy and the difficult decision that they had yet to make. He felt she had been through enough already and needed to try to relax and give her wounds time to heal.

He told her that he was returning to the hotel to deal with whatever was needed of him there and also to get a much-needed bath and some clean clothes. Both were essential after several days at her bedside. They hugged and he quietly left, informing the staff that he would very shortly return. He finally requested that they inform him by telephone if there was any change at all in her condition.

Kokee was now toper most of his mind, having overtaken any plans for their hotel, his recruits or his scheme to regain 'his' casino. That was not so, however, for many other local residents.

Following several days of torrential rains, the swollen Naranjo River in Guatemala City burst its banks at 2 am one morning. It sent a deluge of mud right through the shanty town of Dias es Fiel and down into the valley directly below. It engulfed a local school in seconds without warning. It was completely destroyed. The only consolation was that, because it was a Sunday, nobody was in it, so thankfully, no lives were lost there that morning.

Others in a nearby area were not so lucky. Eventually, it transpired that twenty-one people had died, seven of them being children, buried alive sleeping in their beds. A dreadful disaster for so many families.

One distraught grieving resident, who wanted to remain anonymous, told the local newspaper, the *Prensa Libre*, that whilst he had seen landslides before, he never expected one to take his whole family. It was truly a heartbreaking story to read.

There had been many similar occurrences in recent times, some ten thousand homes, along with many roads and bridges, had been destroyed in just the previous year alone. However often it happened, residents never were able to get used to or understand it.

On his arrival back at Pathways, Antonio was immediately accosted by some of his team, eagerly wanting to know how Kokee was. Over the past weeks, they all had become attached to them both as real friends and their concern was genuine. He updated them as best he could, taking into account his rather confused state of mind at this time. In reality, he was in a bad place right now. He had lost all sight of the mission he was previously so focused on and wasn't even thinking about the disaster the mudslide had caused. All he could think about was Kokee and why this had happened.

He was now taking on board the facts that he had been given but not earlier fully absorbed. Namely, Kokee was hit as she leant across him. It was clear to the police that the bullet was meant for him and now he was finally realising this for himself.

He was contacted by phone and also received visits from many of his guests all wanting to know how Kokee was. One of them, an old friend of Kokee, Diego, who was sitting at the back, told him what he had already told the police, namely that he saw two men, dressed in black, running to a small white car—one with a rather noisy, likely defective, exhaust.

This really woke Antonio up. He remembered that the remaining two casino owners did indeed have a small, ageing white car. He remembered that he had always wondered why they never bought something better with the money they clearly were making.

Armed with this piece of information, he visited the local police station, where he met the senior detective assigned to this high-profile case. His name was Mateo Castro. He imparted his information, telling him that two of the owners of the local casino, Rafael and Sergio, not only had a tangible motive but also owned a rather old white car.

This now gave the police a vital new lead and they promised to check out these two characters and their car straight away.

Antonio went back to his hotel. Momentarily having completely forgotten why he had returned, leaving Kokee alone in the hospital. He finally got a shower and some much-needed fresh clothes.

After informing his trusty band of recruits that no further work was required from them for the time being, he retired to his room. Exhausted, he lay on his bed for what he thought would be just a few moments. He promptly fell into a deep sleep. Considering how little rest he had managed whilst holding vigil beside Kokee's bed, this was certainly not surprising.

Chapter 27

Some four hours later, he awakened with a start. His mobile was ringing, a sound that in previous days had usually been a welcome sign that a friend was reaching out to him. Today, it not only startled him but scared him too. *Was it bad news?*

He answered it rapidly with trepidation. To his relief, it was the local mayor, not the hospital.

After first asking after Kokee, he informed Antonio of the disaster that had demolished the local infants school, leaving twenty-three small children, all under five years of age, with nowhere for their three-hour morning school. Antonio already had been informed of this but was so preoccupied with Kokee that he hadn't thought about it very much. The mayor, whilst understanding what Antonio was going through at this time, still asked if he had any space in his hotel that could be temporarily utilised as somewhere that the children to use for the time being.

Antonio, still in some shock and groggy from both the sedatives he had taken and also from his sleep, informed him he would check out the possibilities and call him back after he had discussed it with Kokee. He got dressed and returned to the hospital.

A short while later, he was again back at Kokee's bedside; she was asleep.

He sat beside her, quietly holding her hand. After only a short while, she stirred and smiled at her husband. Once she had fully come to, she began chatting normally with him. Antonio noticed straight away that she seemed a little brighter; although she did complain of lower pelvic pain which reappeared whenever the morphine she was periodically taking wore off.

Now realising that she was completely in possession of all her faculties and able to fully understand more of the situation, he told her all he now knew.

Kokee showed no surprise at his revelation about her pregnancy, because of course she already knew this. She listened carefully to all he told her about the lodged bullet and the horrible choice they had to make. As soon as she realised this, she cried.

She told him she thought for sure that she was expecting but wanted to wait until the pregnancy was three months in advance before saying anything. She clearly wanted to be sure all was well. Now, it was clear that all was going to be far from well. She sobbed and he hugged her, crying too. They remained like this, motionless, for several minutes before either spoke. Antonio said, "We have to both agree on a decision and inform the doctor, but there is not an immediate rush today. Right now, you must get your strength back; you have not only been through a big ordeal but a massive shock too. We will get through this together. You are young, in good health, and we are both strong."

He then continued. "Your old friend, Diego, was sitting at the back row of our guests and was able to give the police what was probably the most useful piece of information. He saw two men running away behind him immediately after the shot was taken. He saw them run to a small white car and drive away at speed. He wasn't able to describe either of these men, who were dressed in black with hoods, or the car in any real detail; however, he did notice it was very noisy, most likely from a defective exhaust!"

Kokee said, "How could that help?"

Antonio replied, "I know the two now running the casino had a small white car and I have informed the police of this additional fact. They are interviewing them, most likely at this very moment. They will certainly inspect their car too."

He then took a short list of things that Kokee needed whilst confined to the hospital and left to return to Pathways and his duties there. He promised to return first thing the following morning.

She kissed him and he left. She lay for at least two hours before sleeping again. She had the dilemma of the decision they had to make running around in her head before doing so.

Antonio had not yet told Kokee about the tragedy of the mudslide, deciding she didn't need any further burden at this time.

The school and what to do about the little children were going over and over in his mind. He could accommodate them, of course, but it would conflict with his work of training his team. Where should his priorities lie on this and on Kokee's unborn child too? He took a large brandy to bed and was soon again fast asleep.

Chapter 28

He was awakened by loud voices downstairs. He quickly put some clothes on and went down. There he was greeted by Mateo, the detective heading the attempted murder case. He explained that he had interviewed the suspects, Rafael and Sergio, but they denied any knowledge of the events and again cited being at their friend's bar as an alibi. This was conveniently confirmed by the owner in his statement. The police told Antonio that they were most sceptical as to its truth.

Mateo was able to confirm that they did indeed have a small white car parked outside but couldn't inspect it as they wished, due to not yet having a search warrant. He told Antonio that these two were firmly the prime suspects, he just had to get enough evidence to make a case that could convict either of them. He went on to say that they were applying for this vital search warrant but warned that it could take a few days or even weeks to be approved. His concern was that vital evidence could vanish in that time and the trail could go cold. For this reason, he stressed the urgency of this search to the issuing authorities. They all would now need to be patient.

After collecting together the things Kokee had requested he bring for her, he again returned to the hospital. He found her sitting up reading a newspaper. She beamed from ear to ear on seeing him. She told him she had slept well and was feeling much better; he could see straight away that she certainly looked brighter. Kokee then announced that she had something important to tell him.

"I have given careful thought as to what should be done about the bullet and our unborn baby. If you can agree, I would like to decline any operation and take my chances with future mobility. I want to protect our baby. Can you agree with this decision?"

Antonio was stunned by this and gasped, "No, I don't believe I can. Your health and our life together is my priority. I think we should have this bullet removed in order to give you the best opportunity of a full recovery." So, whilst they both agreed to further discuss the predicament with their doctor and to continue to keep open minds, they left this discussion there for the moment.

They then changed the subject to talk about the disastrous mud landslide and the devastation it had caused. Kokee already had learnt something of it, having just read the morning's news in their local paper.

Antonio then proposed a radical conclusion he had arrived at. This time, it was something they were both able to agree on.

He explained that this shooting and injury inflicted upon Kokee had made him rethink his priorities. He told her that without her, he felt he would have nothing. She was clearly his soul mate, his life. The casino and money had suddenly slid into insignificance compared. He told her that he was willing to release the team of recruits, abandon the retaking of the casino, and concentrate on their future together. There were tears in his eyes as he told her all this. On agreeing with him, she welled up in tears too. She readily agreed and he lay beside her. They hugged and hugged. It was wonderful to see the clear and deep love that they shared.

On returning to their hotel, he wrote a letter which politely summoned all his remaining team, seven of them, to meet at 8 am the following morning in the usual room. It simply said that an important announcement would be made that would affect them all. It was printed and distributed to all their rooms during the evening.

He felt the decision he and Kokee had made, just about to be announced, was a load off his shoulders. He felt things could only go up from here.

He placed an order to his kitchen staff for his favourite dinner—slices of honey-glazed ham with mashed potato and onion gravy.

He also ordered a bottle of 'Faustino 1', a fruity red Spanish wine; it was his favourite. He suddenly felt positive, secretly believing that he would succeed in persuading Kokee to have that all-important operation, one that would give her a full and active life together with him. He didn't yet know that this persuasion of a strong woman was going to be far from easy.

At 8 am prompt, all seven of the team were waiting for him in the room adjoining the dining area. They were all confused and concerned as to what Antonio was about to say.

He arrived just a few moments later to find seven eager pairs of ears. He began, with what was so profound, it moved several of them to tears, or at least to lumps in their throats.

"You all know what happened at my birthday party and the serious injury that was inflicted on my Kokee. The purpose of this get-together this morning is three-fold."

"Firstly to tell you that both Kokee and I appreciate all you have done for us and that we have come to view you more as friends than employees. Secondly, I want to fully update you with all I can at the moment. The police have excellent leads as to the perpetrators of this evil attempted murder, a killing that has now become clear was intended for me. They will surely bring them to justice, hopefully very soon now. Kokee is injured but expected to make a full recovery in time. Patience is needed here. Thirdly, and most important for you all is a decision Kokee and I came to just this afternoon. Namely, this dreadful event has made us both realise where our priorities lie…and it is not with casinos nor with money. It is with our lives together."

"So, we have decided to permanently abandon our plans to regain the casino and to, instead, concentrate on our time together, being grateful for what we have, rather than looking for more, or seeking soul-consuming revenge. You are, therefore, all released from your roles of working for us. You can collect your passports and leave as you like. Should you choose to stay here at Pathways for the time being, whilst you decide on your plans, you are of course more than welcome to take your time in doing so. Kokee and I both wish you all a good future with a fresh start. We hope we have helped you each on that journey."

There was silence in the room; you could have heard a pin drop. Everyone was stunned and moved by this speech. It was, of course, good news for them all, although not all knew at this stage where they would go and exactly what they would do.

Antonio went to take a little light breakfast with something of a spring in his step. He felt he was moving forward positively at last. He did, however, need to agree on the way forward with Kokee as far as the operation to remove the bullet was concerned. He was convinced that doing this was the most sensible thing to do. However, would she ever agree?

Chapter 29

After only a few days, the police got the search warrant that they were so keen to obtain. It had been fast-tracked under the circumstances of an attempted murder case. Something that hadn't happened locally before in anyone's living memory.

Three detectives visited Sergio's home that same day. Despite a very thorough search, no evidence whatsoever to link them to the crime was found. Furthermore, what was most surprising was that there was no fault with the exhaust system of their white Opel car. They did, however, note that the silencer appeared to be quite new. They left, disappointed at what seemed to have been a dead end.

Antonio again returned to the hospital. Instead of going directly to Kokee's bedside, he requested the possibility of a private meeting with her doctor. Antonio was in luck, the doctor was able to come to see him straight away as he was on a short break. Just a few minutes later, he duly appeared. Antonio was taken through to a private room. After thanking the doctor for his time and the care he was affording his wife, he asked for a full assessment of the situation. He wanted to know the probabilities involved with both options, to operate or not.

The doctor explained, "There are no guarantees or certainties, all I can do is give you my considered opinion. I believe that if we operate and remove the bullet, your wife will have at least an eighty per cent chance of full mobility and be free from pain after a short time, probably just a few weeks. I do believe, however, that there is little doubt that the pregnancy will terminate and the foetus will be aborted." This was broadly in line with what had already been said, albeit that this was rather more specific.

He went on, "However, should you choose to refuse this operation, then not only will she suffer quite severe pain for a considerable period, possibly permanently, but she also is most unlikely to be able to walk properly, if at all, for the rest of her life." He then added a new piece of information, the most concerning one. "There is also a very real possibility that if left the bullet will decay inside her body, and then serious infection and subsequent complications could possibly occur. It is my firm advice that she has this operation sooner rather than later if you want her to have the full recovery that I believe she can achieve."

Antonio again thanked him for all this, shook his hand warmly, and promised to discuss it all further with Kokee, with a view to a decision very soon. He didn't say anything about Kokee's current reluctance to have this surgery. He was still hopeful he could persuade her to agree to this course of action.

During the following days, many discussions took place between them at the bedside on this dilemma. Despite her continued pain, Kokee remained stubbornly determined to save the pregnancy and steadfastly stated she did not want any operation that would risk her baby.

Meanwhile, a meeting took place at the local police station to discuss where they were with the investigation of this crime. Two ideas came from their discussions. Firstly to check in the town with the local garage concerning the new-looking silencer fitted to Sergio's car, and secondly, a check at the sports and gunsmith dealer nearby for any recent local sales of guns or ammunition. It was agreed either or both could make a real difference. They, like Antonio, were convinced of the pair's guilt; it was obtaining enough evidence to charge them that was the challenge.

Armed with photos of both suspects, visits were made to investigate these two businesses.

The local garage quickly produced a result. They were easily able to confirm that they did indeed replace the silencer on Sergio's car quite recently. On checking the invoice date, it showed to have been carried out the day after the shooting. Furthermore, the owner remembered that Sergio had insisted it be done immediately as it had become urgent, following a warning from the police due to the considerable noise it was making when he was stopped recently.

The detectives were quickly able to ascertain that no record of any noise warning by the police had been given. It was crystal clear what the real reason for the urgent repair was. They were attempting to cover their tracks. This, whilst just another small piece of the jigsaw they were putting together, was not sufficient evidence to yet charge them. It was, however, enough to further fuel their motivation to keep digging.

Their visit to the sports shop was not so enlightening. On being questioned about recent gun and ammunition sales, the owner could only confirm that no rifle had been sold during the past three months at least. He did, however, confirm frequent sales of cartridges for rifles. As the police had no knowledge of the kind of rifle used, the type of ammunition was also unknown.

They showed pictures of the two suspects to the owner. He called his assistant to look at them also. He said that, whilst he couldn't be certain, he had sold a box of ammunition to a man looking something like Sergio, for a Remmington rifle a few weeks back. He was, however, not one hundred per cent sure of his identity. He did confirm the date of the sale of a single box of cartridges as just six days before the shooting had taken place. Whilst the police were gradually piecing it together, they still had the major obstacle of the pair's alibi to contend with. They, however, just did not believe it.

The following morning, they brought the restaurant owner in for questioning. He made a statement confirming that the pair had been in his restaurant at the time of the shooting, however the times stated in this interview conflicted with those given earlier. This in itself was no proof of anything but did further confirm the detectives' suspicion that he was lying to protect his friends. They made this very clear to him. He left the police station that day with increasing anxiety as to his involvement and implication in this crime. He felt sure he was getting deeper into something he wasn't comfortable with at all.

Back at the police station, armed with these new pieces of information, a further meeting took place. The senior detective, Mateo Castro, outlined what they now knew.

1. The suspects, Sergio and Rafael, had a very strong motive.
2. They had a reliable witness to testify that he saw two men in black running away to a small white car. One that clearly had a defective exhaust.
3. The suspects' small white car had received a new silencer straight after the shooting.
4. Sergio had lied about the reason for the urgency of the repairs to the exhaust.
5. Someone matching Sergio's appearance had purchased a small box of rifle ammunition the week before the shooting.
6. There were discrepancies in the alibi timing provided by the restaurant owner in two completely separate statements.

Based on all this, the question was, did they have enough to charge the pair?

They decided that they may just have enough and promptly arrested the pair on suspicion of the crime.

They were read their rights and separately interrogated for nine hours, hoping for some kind of breakthrough.

They were looking for a confession or for further evidence from confused statements. Unfortunately, no concrete progress was made at all and there was finally no choice but to release them both without charge.

Meanwhile, the restaurant's owner was becoming increasingly concerned at the police line of questioning and wanted to distance himself from the whole thing. He had been hiding the rifle and the remaining bullets for Sergio, who had realised that his home would be likely for a search.

He was keen to be rid of them as soon as possible. He decided he would insist they be urgently removed from his premises. He subsequently called Sergio and told him that he wanted to see him that evening in the restaurant. Sergio agreed to visit for dinner at 8 pm.

Chapter 30

Days, which felt more like weeks, passed, with Antonio still visiting Kokee twice a day but making no progress on their big decision. They simply could not agree.

The seven recruits were all privately making their plans but still were all residing at their comfortable hotel. One they were now paying for; albeit at a very reasonable mates' rate!

The police, having weighed up all the evidence they had, decided it was circumstantial and insufficient to make a charge. They were, of course, frustrated but had no other stones to look under at this time.

But then, out of the blue, an astonishing turn of events occurred. A local resident who had been away travelling in the USA for a few weeks returned. He renewed his relationship with his favourite restaurant by going there for dinner on his first day home. He sat in a corner in his usual spot and ordered a drink. The restaurant was empty at this early part of the evening, so he just relaxed, unwinding from both his travels and the jetlag that had started to kick in.

He couldn't see who it was that came in at 8 pm, but he could overhear some parts of a conversation between him and the owner. It was about a rifle and ammunition. Details of the conversation were sparse, but in a slightly raised voice, the owner was clearly heard to say, "Take them away from here, do it now."

The man replied, "I'll take the gun, but you get rid of the cartridges."

Having been away for several weeks, this resident knew nothing of the local shooting crime and didn't understand what it was all about. He stood up, just in time to get a glimpse of the man from behind as he was leaving, carrying a sizeable bag. He wasn't able to recognise this individual from behind as someone local that he knew, but could clearly see he was of a slight build and was quite tall.

He left the restaurant when he had eaten his dinner a couple of hours later and thought nothing more of what he had overheard and, in any event, this was none of his business anyway.

It was a couple of days later that this local resident, Hugo Garcia, was finally catching up with the local news in the past two issues of the *Prensa Libra*, their local newspaper, that his jaw dropped and he froze in his chair. He couldn't believe what he had just read.

Firstly, he was, of course, deeply troubled by the mudslide the area had experienced; he had no idea about its occurrence.

Secondly, in the other copy of their paper, he read about the assassination attempt on a local hotel owner. Something else he was learning for the first time. He was more than stunned.

He was quickly putting together this crime with what he had overheard in the restaurant. Suddenly, it dawned on him that surely there was a connection.

However, his first thought was for those who had perished in the mudslide, so he immediately called a good friend for more details. Whilst it was tragic that so many had lost their lives, he was at least slightly relieved to learn their identities; he knew none of them personally. His next move was to visit the local police station where, on explaining his reasons, he was quickly put in front of one of the detectives handling the investigation into the shooting, something that had occurred whilst he had been away travelling overseas.

He told this detective what he had overheard and seen on his visit to the local restaurant. Whilst what he had heard was clear, he couldn't really identify the man concerned.

All he could say was that he was of a slight build with short dark hair. Also, he was of above-average height. After he had made a written statement, he was thanked and he left.

The details of this interview and the resulting statement were immediately communicated to Mateo Castro. Despite being on a day off, he immediately returned to the station. After further discussions and everything being thoroughly digested, a new search warrant was applied for. Its urgency again was stressed.

The following morning, it duly arrived. This case was clearly getting every possible resource from the authorities. Armed with the new warrant, they again paid Sergio a visit. Again, three of them.

It didn't take long before the rifle was found in an old cupboard in the basement. They wrapped it in a large plastic bag, taking care not to handle it or mark it in any way. Sergio was again arrested and taken directly to the police station for the further questioning this find had now prompted.

He was taken into an interview room and informed that this interview was being recorded. Under caution, he was again interrogated at length.

After some four hours, all they could add to what they already knew: Yes, he owned the rifle and also held a licence to do so. He claimed he had bought it for hunting but had not yet used it, pointing out that he as yet had no ammunition. He did confirm it was only recently purchased online.

This was, of course, contrary to what they now knew but they didn't want to display their full hand at the moment, so didn't pursue any further questioning on the ammunition with him at this time, nor what had prompted this second search. He was then released.

Mateo, accompanied by a second detective, again visited the restaurant and arrested the owner for questioning on suspicion of aiding and abetting a serious crime. He was trembling as he was put into the back of the police car and whisked away to the station. During the time that followed, he managed to calm his nerves. After all, he knew that he had already got rid of both the gun and, shortly after, the ammunition too, so he felt confident that there was no evidence against him. Under questioning, he simply denied any knowledge of the rifle and of any discussion with Sergio about one.

As he steadfastly stuck to this statement, there was little more the police could do at this stage. They released him without charge.

Chapter 31

The police contacted their forensic department in the city and requested them visit to collect the rifle for a detailed examination and for a written report. Within a couple of hours, someone arrived and, after showing his credentials, was allowed to take the suspected weapon away, along with copies of Sergio's fingerprints that they had previously taken. The man promised a speedy evaluation of this rifle, whose fingerprints were on it and a check to ascertain whether it had been used, and if so, how recently.

The police were gradually building a case against both Sergio and the restaurant owner, Benjamin. They did, however, realise much of their evidence so far was largely circumstantial. They knew to be confident of the conviction that they were now becoming sure was needed, would need more concrete evidence.

Kokee had now regained her strength and was almost ready to be discharged from the hospital. Antonio, together with her doctor, again made a strong case to Kokee for the urgent removal of the bullet. Their arguments again fell on deaf ears. She still clung to her earlier decision to wait until her baby was born, despite the fact that this was months away and that she would likely suffer permanent damage by waiting that long before surgery.

Antonio continued to be disappointed at her stubbornness but knew nothing more could be done on this issue without her written consent. He returned to Pathways to find that Mateo Castro had left a message for him to return to the station for an update on their progress thus far. The message said he was at the station all day and would make himself available for Antonio at any time convenient to him.

After checking all was in order at the hotel, he left for the police station, only stopping briefly on the way for some provisions he urgently needed.

On arrival at the station, he was directed to a small private interview room. He only had to wait a few moments before Mateo arrived. They warmly shook hands and sat facing each other across a small table, one more often used for interviewing suspects of crime.

He fully updated Antonio on all that they now knew. He told him of the witness from the restaurant that had come forward and the subsequent finding and seizure of the rifle. He explained that whilst this was the most significant piece of evidence so far, it didn't yet prove anything. It was just another piece of a large jigsaw. He stressed that it was vital that Antonio make no contact with the witness who had overheard this conversation in the restaurant. He also strongly advised him that he should not visit the restaurant again for the time being. He pointed out that discussions with either person could jeopardise the later process of law. Antonio communicated that he understood and would comply with this.

Mateo finally told him that the remaining piece of missing evidence that could surely prove without doubt Sergio's guilt was being able to match the bullet to his gun. Antonio explained that so far, Kokee had refused the operation needed to remove the bullet from the base of her spine due to the very real risk to her baby. However, armed with what Mateo had said, he promised to use this to try harder to persuade her how important the surgery had now become. He left the station feeling substantially encouraged that real progress was now being made.

On returning to his hotel, he ordered a late luncheon from the kitchen of patatas bravas, a very popular Spanish dish of shallow fried potato cubes served with a spicy sauce. Something he knew his chef could prepare quickly at short notice. After eating this meal, he called the town hall and left a message for the mayor to call him, when convenient, to discuss the problem of the twenty-three infants with no school to go to.

Antonio had been giving much thought to everything that had happened like a whirlwind in these recent days. Kokee lying in the hospital narrowly escaping death had made him seriously rethink his priorities. The lost casino now seemed insignificant in the scale of things.

Perhaps, it was time to focus his plans on things closer to home.

The mayor phoned the following morning and Antonio requested a slot in his busy diary to meet and discuss the lost school and the possibility of some assistance for the little children. An appointment was set for the following Monday when the mayor would meet with him at Pathways.

Antonio again returned to the hospital.

Kokee was even brighter today and told him she had taken her first steps out of bed and, although rather painful, she was able to walk unaided. She said the doctor was to visit her later that morning to discuss her progress.

She further told him that she was hopeful of a discharge very soon.

She quietly informed Antonio that she was fed up with being stuck there as she missed his company and in addition, she was craving some quality food. She whispered, "If ever we lose our hotel chef, don't employ the hospital one!"

Within a few minutes, the doctor arrived at her bedside. He was carrying a chart and a file. "How are we both today?" He asked. Kokee said that she was feeling better and was strong enough to walk a little now. Antonio enquired on her behalf as to when she could be discharged into his care at their home.

The doctor told them that if she was not having the operation to remove the bullet at this time, she could leave that very afternoon after a final check and sign-off by the senior nurse who had tirelessly looked after her. This was music to their ears. The final appointment with this nurse was to be not for another hour or so. Antonio, therefore, told her he would risk a coffee and a cake in the hospital's café whilst he waited for this nurse to complete her work in examining Kokee for the last time.

Antonio was pleasantly surprised that both the coffee and cake he selected were rather good, contrary to Kokee's assessment of the hospital's culinary efforts. He wondered if perhaps the cakes were made outside the hospital and just bought in.

On returning to Kokee's ward, he found screens around her bed clearly there to afford privacy, so he sat close by and patiently waited. After only a few minutes, the screens were removed by a nurse to reveal Kokee sitting on the end of her bed fully dressed, complete with comfortable-looking shoes. It seemed the screens were not due to any intimate checking of her wound but were there whilst the nurse helped her to get dressed. So, now, she was at last ready to be taken home.

On arriving at the hotel, Kokee was most surprised to be greeted by a group of people applauding her. Unknown to her, Antonio had called from the hospital café to alert them she was coming back momentarily. So, they were there all prepared to give her this warm welcome. They obviously held her in high regard and with a sincere fondness. It moved her to tears. They all sat together in the lounge and enjoyed a glass or two of sparkling, ice-cold cava. She was so happy to be home again after such an ordeal. After thanking everyone for the warm welcome she had been given, she excused herself to take some more rest. It had been a tiring day for her thus far.

Chapter 32

Antonio took this opportunity to remind his trusty recruits that nothing further would be asked of them. He was giving up the plan concerning the casino for good and they were all free to go anywhere they pleased. They already appreciated that this was the case, based on what Antonio had previously said. Some had not given much thought to future plans but some already had.

Peter had been looking online at management opportunities in UK companies. He was searching in the areas of Devon and Dorset, avoiding anywhere near his previous company in Berkshire. He created a fake CV under his new name and applied for several different positions. Mostly sales and marketing ones which were the most closely aligned with his past experience. He claimed to have been out of the UK for many years, working in Guatemala. He felt that Antonio, together with his forger friend, could assist him with a suitable reference.

Time passed with little or no positive response to these applications. They either declined an interview or, in some cases, didn't even reply. Peter found it most frustrating as it was clearly going to prove more difficult than he had anticipated to escape, with something to escape to.

Joanna was undecided as to what to do. She knew that she couldn't be exposed publically as a model in the UK, as she would surely be quickly recognised, but she really had little other work experience to fall back on. She was, however, reasonably content with her work at the casino; she quite enjoyed the job. It was living at the hotel in Guatemala she wanted to get away from.

She was talking with Peter about this dilemma when he made a suggestion. He said, "You have stated that you enjoy the buzz of the casino work, but are bored with this quiet area, so why not look further afield for similar work?" He went on to tell her that he had spent a very enjoyable couple of nights at a lovely hotel in Las Vegas which had a large, very busy casino. Also, the nightlife was vibrant everywhere there, something that would surely suit her. He also pointed out that Antonio had told him that he had spent time there on his honeymoon; a rather longer stay than his and he would therefore know even more about the hotels and life there. She was pleased with this advice and decided to talk to Antonio when convenient for them both.

Monday came and the mayor arrived for his appointment with Antonio to discuss the schooling of the small children.

Antonio was taken a bit by surprise as he had not only failed to discuss it with Kokee but had actually forgotten all about this scheduled meeting. He showed him into a private room, served him the coffee he had chosen, and asked his indulgence for a few minutes whilst he fetched Kokee to join them.

Almost immediately, the three of them were all together to discuss the problem that these infants and their parents faced. Antonio was more than relieved and delighted that Kokee readily supported the idea that had already been provisionally agreed by Antonio; namely that their hotel be used to house these children for a few hours a week.

The mayor explained that the parents all paid for this schooling and that, even after paying the three staff and necessary insurance, it was a profitable venture and they would be willing to pay for the hotel facilities. Both of them quickly agreed that they didn't need to pay for what they were offering, other than perhaps a small contribution to overheads such as drinks for the children and any other consumables used. The mayor was more than satisfied with this. To further support this cause, Kokee offered her services to look after the children without reward of any kind.

This was all more than the mayor, the children, the parents, or indeed the community could have possibly expected. After the mayor left, they had a little quiet time alone and, whilst Kokee seemed in such good positive spirits, Antonio chose this moment to again broach the subject of the bullet lodged in her spine.

He outlined in detail everything the police had told him and all the evidence they currently had. It all pointed towards Sergio but it was clear that it was only circumstantial so far and that they were most unsure that they yet had enough evidence to obtain the conviction they so badly wanted. He told her that the thing that could surely seal the case would be a positive matching of the hidden bullet to Sergio's rifle. Without it, they really had reached a dead end. He again begged her to have it removed with the virtual certainty of justice being done. He said it could offer complete closure for all involved.

In light of this explanation, she agreed to reconsider and promised to sleep on it. They enjoyed some pleasant together time for the rest of the day. They had a lovely dinner together and watched one of their favourite films before retiring to bed for an early night. They fell asleep, almost at the same time, in each other's arms. Nobody in earshot of their room told either of them but they both snored contently in a deep sleep together.

Chapter 33

The following morning, Joanna got the opportunity she was looking for to speak with Antonio regarding his experiences in Las Vegas. She explained that she was considering the possibility of living and working there. He was able to confirm straight away what Peter had said and was able to give her a list of several hotels and casinos there. He stressed that these were just the ones he could remember, pointing out that there were a great many to choose from in a relatively small area. He assured her that he didn't think employment there would be hard to find.

He did, however, say that she may have to start off as a waitress before gaining the opportunity of running a table as she was doing now. Joanna thanked him and went through to the dining room for her usual healthy fruit and coffee breakfast.

Antonio and Kokee spent considerable time discussing the option of an operation to remove the bullet. There was a great deal at stake for all involved. Her main questions to Antonio were as to whether the doctor had said it was certain the foetus would be aborted or whether it was just a strong possibility. Also, if she did lose this pregnancy, would it have any effect on a future opportunity for having a child? He told her that he wasn't one hundred per cent certain as to the answer to either question and that they should go to the hospital and again consult the doctor on these important points. They agreed to go the following day if an appointment with the doctor could be obtained.

Antonio found it hard to hide his pleasure that finally she seemed to be coming around to his way of thinking. He was determined that Kokee have the chance of a full mobile life and not suffer pain or disability of any kind. He called the hospital to find that their doctor was on a two-day break and wouldn't be back until Thursday. The receptionist was, however, able to confirm a slot in his diary for 2 pm on that day. They would have no choice but to wait just one more day for this vital discussion; one Antonio passionately wanted in order to have the positive conclusion of a date for this operation.

They both kept themselves busy for these two days by dismantling their home casino to make way for the children's 'school'. The senior teacher of the group was invited to visit the facility to discuss what equipment would be required.

She arrived promptly that afternoon, not wanting to miss this wonderful opportunity of somewhere to continue their work with these young children.

She introduced herself as Lola Linde. She told them the background of this private school.

"As a teacher and a mother myself, I realised that children waiting until they were five or six before being able to start school here was not best for either the children or for their mothers needing to work. So, with the aid of a small government grant and some savings, I started this school eight years ago with just five children, including my two-year-old daughter. Since then, we have grown into a profitable little business offering a worthwhile service to the local community. So much so that we are now legally registered as a charity and we receive an annual grant to help us. This grant paid for the rental of the facility that, along with all our equipment, is now in ruins."

"It is uncertain as to whether this grant will continue to be offered in the future now. Is it true that you are offering your premises at no charge?" Antonio confirmed, except for any refreshments, that this was the case. Furthermore, he told her that Kokee would like to offer her help to look after the children, also at no cost to the 'school'. Lola was delighted to hear all this.

The discussions for the next hour or so concerned the equipment they needed to replace. Lola explained that their insurance did not cover these mudslides that were unfortunately all too common in the area. So, she was in the process of buying what was needed, using some of the capital in the business and more from donations from the local community. She had a list of the things that were needed. Some had been ordered and were scheduled to be delivered within a week. There were several other items that had not yet been arranged.

Antonio and Kokee studied this list of requirements, none were likely to prove expensive or difficult to obtain, so they told Lola straight away that they would provide them as a donation. Lola was delighted to hear this. She told them that she was planning on opening this new school in ten days' time if acceptable to them. This was readily confirmed by them both and a date was set. With that, she thanked them profusely and left with a spring in her step. She realised that the community was lucky to have such kind people in their midst.

After she had left, they immediately got on with preparing the required area for the children. This included some redecorating of part of the room. They made arrangements with a local person to do this work. They then left for town to purchase the items that had been outstanding on Lola's list. All were likely to be readily available and would ensure all was ready for the scheduled opening day.

Chapter 34

Thursday afternoon at 2 pm prompt found Antonio and Kokee at the hospital for their arranged appointment with the doctor. They were, however, informed that he had been diverted unexpectedly for an emergency and would be delayed for a short while; an hour at most they were told.

They decided that it wasn't worth going away and returning for such a short time and therefore informed his secretary that they would be waiting in the hospital's cafeteria. She agreed to call his mobile as soon as she could. They departed to the far wing of the hospital where this was located. They each ordered coffee and slices of chocolate cake.

The wait was in reality only about forty minutes but seemed longer as they were so anxious for answers to their questions. They returned to the doctor's office and sat before his large mahogany desk.

Straight away, Kokee told him that she had given further thought as to the possibility of the bullet's removal and may now be willing to accept his recommendation to carry out this procedure.

She outlined her two main questions: firstly, whether losing the baby was virtually certain or just a possibility, and secondly, whether the operation could have any effect on achieving a future successful pregnancy.

He started with a positive. He told them that the chances of the operation having any detrimental effect on her conceiving again were most unlikely, indeed virtually guaranteed. This was the good news.

He then addressed her first question as to the effect on the current pregnancy. He pulled no punches as he warned her that aborting the baby was almost a certainty. He explained that it was unlikely to be avoided. Although this was the bad news that they were expecting, it still wasn't what they wanted to hear. Antonio put his arm around Kokee as she cried.

After a few moments of silence, the doctor asked the couple if they would like some time to discuss this decision alone. They looked at each other and both told him, "No, it must be done, so we agree with what has been your recommendation all along." The doctor was delighted and promised to get back to them with a date for the operation when he had consulted his diary and that of the operating theatre. In any event, he promised it would only be a few days hence as he considered this operation urgent.

Meanwhile, at Pathways, all the redundant recruits were now giving serious thought as to where they were going and what they would next be doing.

Joanna was happy with Michael but didn't want to stay in Guatemala. She outlined her aspirations to him for a casino job in Las Vegas. The question she had to ask was whether he would go with her if she packed and left. This unexpected question took him a little aback and off guard. His initial reaction was confusion. He had thought they were content as they were and he also was thinking about his father. He promised to think about it and also to discuss it with him.

Joanna, feeling fairly sure he would agree eventually, started contacting airlines for flight routes and prices. She also made written contact with several of the large casino hotels on the Strip, as it was known locally.

After several disappointing responses to Peter's job applications in the UK, he was delighted to receive a positive one from a company in Poole, Dorset, that manufactured marine navigation equipment, sonars and the like, for example. The position was one of production manager. The letter offered him an interview just over three weeks hence. He immediately replied to confirm he would attend and asked if they could assist with recommendations of local hotels where he could stay for a few days. He then checked out flight availability. He went down to the hotel bar and ordered a large gin and tonic. He was in great spirits.

When Antonio was reading the weekly *Prensa Libra* newspaper, he was shocked. There was a small article about a certain Matt Bradbury, better known to him only as Matt Dunbar. He had been arrested and charged with an offence of indecent sexual behaviour towards two thirteen-year-old twin girls. The article didn't name the children, of course, but did say that their single-parent mother had been taking flying lessons with him at his school. The offences seemed serious and, knowing Guatemala's laws and standards, Antonio felt certain he would receive a custodial sentence.

This would be likely, even though the police would have no way of linking him to his former name and the similar crime he had run away from. It seemed that he hadn't learnt from his mistakes and that Karma had finally caught up with him. Secretly, Antonio had little sympathy for him.

George and Wan had become good friends and spent quite a bit of time together. George was comfortable with his substantial lottery win and his time on the golf course, where he was becoming quite an accomplished player, however, he wanted more.

Wan similarly was comfortable with his financial position now he seemed to have shaken off the UK taxmen. He also was really enjoying his red Ferrari. But, like George, he wanted an interest. One evening, they gave the casino some thought and started to explore the possibility of, together with Antonio, buying it back at a low price. They would then all have an interest. In addition, it was fair to say that Wan at least, and probably George too, were considering buying their own local properties. Both had settled well into the local community and its way of life.

Michael found a convenient time, when having a snooker evening with his father, to discuss the possibility of leaving Guatemala with Joanna to live in Las Vegas. To Michael's surprise and pleasure, his father offered no objection or negative view to this idea. It was clear that he could see his son was happy in his relationship with Joanna and just wanted him to continue with it. Michael decided then and there that he would tell Joanna this news and give the go-ahead to plan for their future in the USA.

He told Joanna that night that he was ready to go with her to Vegas for a really new life together. She was over the moon with excitement because, whilst she had secretly decided to go whatever, she didn't want to break up with him. They had become a real couple. She got back on to flight routes and prices as well as finding a suitable hotel for their initial stay.

It didn't take long. She found reasonably priced flights with United, from Guatemala City Airport to Los Angeles, a six-hour flight, then a short hop to Vegas with the same airline. One-way tickets for both flights were available for as little as $210 each. She booked both for four weeks hence.

Finding a hotel was even easier. She booked the Grand Hotel on the Strip for a week's stay; hopefully, giving enough time to settle in and sort things. They were off! They celebrated with a bottle of cava.

Chapter 35

The following Monday morning brought good news from the hospital. An appointment for Kokee's surgery to remove the lodged bullet had been fixed for Wednesday the following week. Antonio immediately told her this news. Both had mixed emotions but knew it was the right way forward. They, of course, responded in the affirmative as to their agreement to the proposed date and began making their plans around it.

The news Jonathan had received from his son, Michael, about leaving Guatemala for Vegas with Joanna made him think even harder about his own future. He went to the snooker club they had both been frequenting and had a couple of games with another member he knew there. They won a game each. He went to the bar and had a beer with the club's owner. They chatted about the weather, the mudslide, and their lives in general. He told Jonathan that he was finding it difficult to generate sufficient income to keep the club going on snooker and a bar alone. He went on to tell him that he had another substantial area in the club currently being unused and that he was thinking of renting it out for an alternative activity. This gave Jonathan an idea...

He immediately shared this thought with the club owner. He said, "You may remember that I told you that I was a semi-professional boxer with many years of experience. Well, I may be interested in using your space, if suitable, to start a boxing school."

The club manager, Luis, replied, "Yes, I remember, and that is certainly a possibility as far as I am concerned. Would you like to view the space right now?" Jonathan eagerly told him he would. They went together to see the area concerned and he could see straight away that it could be ample for his needs. His only concern was the lack of any secure closure of the area from the rest of the club. Louis told him that, if a rental agreement could be reached, he would be willing to close the area off with a secure locked entrance. This satisfied

Jonathan and he asked Luis to work out a rental rate and whatever contractual details that would be needed.

He left to go and look online for equipment prices; the main ones being the installation of two boxing rings, along with gloves of various sizes, and sundries such as gum shields, etc. He felt very pleased with all this that he had learnt today.

The following day, Peter booked return flights in order to attend his interview in the UK. He also booked a room for three nights at a small hotel on the seafront called 'The Dolphin'. He was pleasantly surprised at the flight prices, but not so with quite unexpectedly expensive accommodation rates. Anyway, it all was a means to an end, so he only complained to himself and made no mention of it to anyone else. He would be away in a few days.

Angela was still missing her home in Scotland; particularly Dundee where she had run away from. She decided she would risk returning to her homeland, but to live in Glasgow where she knew it had a good club nightlife, which would present her with good singing opportunities. She felt that with a different name, a radical hairstyle change, and a distance of about eighty miles, she should be unlikely to be bothered with her past. She too booked a flight to Glasgow, a one-way one, along with a week's stay at a Holiday Inn near the airport.

Gradually, these guests were making and executing their plans to move forward now that their mission had been completed, or rather curtailed. They all agreed on welcoming this.

Wan and George were anxious to discuss a joint venture with Antonio for the casino but realised that, with Kokee's surgery pending, now was not a good time. They, therefore, decided to wait for the right moment.

Chapter 36

Time passed quicker than either Antonio or Kokee could have believed. The day of admission to the hospital for her surgery arrived. The operation was scheduled for the following day.

Because she knew that the hospital stay would be for a few days, Kokee began packing a small case with essential items to take with her. Antonio had already decided he would stay overnight at the hospital, at least until after the operation, so he alerted the hotel staff that he would be away for at least a couple of nights. They had good staff that could be relied on in their absence. A couple of them had been with them for several years and lived in. He felt confident all would be fine in his absence.

The following morning, Kokee and Antonio were both up early and ready to leave in good time, keen not to be late for this important appointment.

Meanwhile, at the hospital, preparations were underway to receive them. Of course, a bed for Kokee, but also one for Antonio in another area set aside for this kind of stay. In addition to the actual operation preparations, arrangements had been made with both the police and reception for the collection of the offending bullet following its removal.

On arrival at the hospital, they were shown to their respective places and each settled in.

After about an hour, the doctor appeared at Kokee's bedside to find her in surprisingly good spirits, reading a book. He explained that in the afternoon she would have a quick medical checkover, blood pressure and temperature tests, for example. He told her that nothing further would be happening until the following morning when the operation was scheduled for 10 am. He also explained that her last food and drinks, until after the operation, would be at 10 pm that evening. She acknowledged her clear understanding of this important sequence of events.

Antonio came and sat with her shortly after the busy doctor had left. They spent the rest of the day together, chatting, possibly a little nervously. They had been assured that, whilst the pending operation was far from a simple routine, it was one not expected to be lengthy, complicated or risky in any way. It was just the survival of the pregnancy that was in question, although they both knew and had accepted the likely outcome.

After hugging her and promising to return first thing the following morning, Antonio left to allow her to eat dinner at 9 pm and went to the canteen to eat something himself.

Looking at the food on offer, he just seemed to lose any inclination to eat at all. It wasn't that there was likely much wrong with their food, but it was more his state of mind, filled with apprehension at the pending operation. He had remained calm and reassuring when he had been with Kokee for her sake, but inside, he was in knots. He barely ate anything but drank a small bottled beer in an attempt to calm his nerves. He then retired to his room and went to his rather uncomfortable bed quite early. After what seemed to be a long time, he eventually got to sleep.

He awoke just before 6 am and got straight up, showered, and dressed. He decided to wait a while to give Kokee some time to prepare herself physically and mentally for the day.

He went to her bedside at 8 am to find her sitting up but rather drowsy. She explained that she had received a pre-med that was responsible. The doctor shortly appeared and, together with a nurse, they left for the operating theatre. He promised to come and report to Antonio after the operation.

Back in his room, that morning was the longest of his life he told friends later. Never had time moved so slowly. He seemed to look at his watch every few minutes which didn't exactly help. A few minutes before 1 pm, the doctor came to his room. Antonio jumped up somewhat startled and filled with trepidation as to what he was about to learn.

He needn't have worried as there was nothing surprising to report. The doctor explained that the operation wasn't as difficult as it may have been and it was a complete success. A success in that the bullet had been removed without complications. He did unfortunately confirm that, as had been expected, the pregnancy had terminated. He was able to assure Antonio that his wife was awake and feeling ok. He did warn him, however, that she was on powerful painkillers that would make her drowsy and not completely communicative. He said he could now visit her but only for a short while as she would need to rest for the remainder of the day.

Antonio was relieved and actually elated to hear these results and left immediately to visit her again. On arrival at her bedside, he found her fast asleep. He didn't know if he was pleased or disappointed at this.

He decided to leave her to regain her strength and went back to his room where he too fell fast asleep.

In the operating theatre, the bullet was put carefully, not cleaned or touched by hand as instructed by the police, into a plastic bag, sealed, and taken to reception awaiting collection.

Somehow, the brothers were informed of all this and Sergio appeared at the hospital reception and told the receptionist he had been sent by the police to collect a sealed packet from them. Without checking any credentials, the small plastic packet was handed over. All he was asked to do was to sign for it. He promptly made an unreadable 'signature' on a form offered to him. With that, he swiftly left the hospital, feeling pleased with the spoils.

Some two hours later, a uniformed police officer arrived at reception and informed the staff there he had come to collect a piece of evidence as had been previously arranged. The puzzled woman on the desk informed the officer that it had already been collected sometime earlier. There then ensued a lengthy discussion between the woman and the manager of this reception facility. After the young woman admitted that she had failed to check the identity of the mystery individual who had walked off with the packet, leaving only a scribble on a piece of paper that was illegible and of no use, the officer informed his superintendent of these events by phone.

Within about thirty minutes, the detective, Mateo Castro, was informed of this disaster and rushed straight to the hospital.

On arrival at the hospital a short while later, he asked for the facilities manager as a matter of urgency. Promptly, he arrived to speak to Mateo, who informed him of what had happened and its significance with regard to a serious crime investigation. He quickly found out that there were several cameras around this reception area and that all would have been recorded…something Sergio had failed to realise.

Once the relevant footage had been reviewed by Mateo, it immediately revealed that the offending person who had absconded with the evidence was indeed Sergio, just as he had suspected.

What was, however, a puzzle at the moment was just how the brothers could have known about this packet being at reception at that exact time. Someone must have informed them, but who?

Unaware of any of this, Antonio awoke and went to Kokee's bedside. This time she was awake, sitting up reading a national newspaper that had been kindly brought in for her by one of the nurses. She was brighter and delighted to see her husband. They hugged, very gently. She told him that the doctor had said the operation was a complete success and that she would be ready to return to her home in two or three days. Antonio echoed this news as the same the doctor had told him earlier. They were so pleased it was all over and didn't dwell any further on the aborted foetus, which was, in reality, only a few weeks old.

Perhaps, they wouldn't have been in quite such good spirits had they known that the vital piece of evidence had been stolen, apparently, so easily.

Her nurse arrived a few minutes later and explained that as Kokee was tired and actually quite weak, he should go home and allow her to get some healing rest. He, of course, agreed straight away, gave her a kiss, and promised to return the following morning first thing.

He left and returned to Pathways. On arrival, he poured himself a large glass of cold cava, before taking a long hot shower and dressing in fresh clothes.

Chapter 37

Mateo took a copy of the security camera's footage as evidence and, together with another officer, they again visited Sergio, this time with an arrest warrant. After reading him his rights, he was arrested and formally charged at the police station with attempted murder. They felt fairly sure now that, with or without the missing bullet, they had a strong enough case to make an attempted murder case succeed in court. Sergio spent most of that day being interrogated but, despite the compelling video evidence from the hospital's camera, he simply denied that the person in the video was him. He was put into a secure cell and left to think overnight as to what he had clearly done.

Mateo called Antonio and, after confirming he was going to be at home for the rest of the day, informed him that he would visit Pathways later that afternoon to update him on all the latest developments. He was also now mindful that, in all the excitement, he had completely forgotten to ask how Kokee's operation had gone and how the brave patient was feeling now she was home again. His first task on arrival at Pathways would surely be that.

But first, together with his staff, he had to get the plan together as to how they would now proceed with this arrest. He promptly applied for an initial hearing at the local law court. This was duly set for just two days hence, well within the legally allowed time to continue holding their prisoner following his having been charged.

Mateo arrived at Pathways around 4 pm that afternoon. He was warmly greeted by both Antonio and Kokee too. He straight away asked her how she was feeling. He was most pleased to hear her tell him that she was feeling really good and very happy to be home again.

The news that the bullet was missing was obviously a big disappointment for them all but once Mateo had assured them that the police were very confident of a successful conviction without it, indeed in stealing it, Sergio had virtually admitted his guilt with this action. At this point, he left and returned to the station to begin the work of putting the whole case together, in readiness for the initial hearing in just two days' time.

The following day was Monday, so Kokee returned to her part-time volunteer work of assisting in the small school now running successfully several days a week.

The children seemed to have settled into their new environment just like nothing had changed.

Jonathan, having received a very reasonable rental contract for his boxing club, was getting on with equipping it with a target of an opening later that month.

Wan and George looked further into the possibility of a joint venture with the casino and even went as far as establishing the likely cost of acquiring it. They, however, didn't bother Antonio with their ideas at this busy time for him. They were content to wait for the moment.

Despite several more attempts to persuade Sergio to admit to the shooting, no further progress was made ahead of the upcoming trial. This, although making the case more difficult, didn't detract from the confidence the police had in a conviction. They just knew it would make the result more time-consuming to achieve.

Chapter 38

The eagerly awaited day of the trial came. The court was in session prompt at 9 am that Wednesday morning. In the gallery were many friends and well-wishers. Antonio's brother, Carlos, even made a surprise visit to be there. He had booked into Pathways with an open-ended stay, clearly interested in seeing the result of the trial. Antonio was not alone in being surprised at this visit, as it was well known that there was not a good brotherly relationship between them. He asked Carlos, "How is the coffee plantation doing?"

He replied, quite curtly, "I sold it two years ago, Antonio! After you left, I found it hard to run it all alone and it got run down and lost its former profit. I was forced to take a low price for it in the end." There was some bitterness in his explanation, clearly resentment that Antonio had left. Whilst Antonio told his brother that he was sorry to hear this news, comments of condolence fell on deaf ears.

The customary three judges entered the court. It was promptly called to session by Judge Franco, the senior of the three. He was someone new to the area and someone not known to most who were present, including Antonio. The other two were longstanding locals, having tried scores of cases over the years.

In Guatemala, there is no jury as in many other countries. Instead the guilt or otherwise is decided by this panel of the three judges. They also, within allowed limits, specify the jail term if appropriate. The purpose of this initial hearing was for these judges to listen to a brief outline of the case by both the prosecution and also the defence.

Their task then was to decide if there was 'probable cause' to go to trial. If so, a date would be set for it to begin.

Judge Franco read out the charge against Sergio, that of attempted murder, and he was asked how he pleaded, guilty or not guilty. As anticipated by everyone, he clearly stated, "Not guilty."

With that, the two opposing lawyers outlined their cases. The defence lawyer only could really state that all the evidence was circumstantial with no solid proof that his client had anything to do with the shooting. This was essentially true, although the prosecuting lawyer stated that his alibis could be disproved by witnesses that would be called at any future trial.

He had to agree that much was circumstantial but that the sheer volume of it was sufficient to warrant the trial they wanted.

The three judges adjourned the court for a two-hour recess for them to deliberate all they had heard.

Whilst nothing could be taken for granted, Antonio's lawyer told him that his considerable experience, particularly his skill of 'reading' judges, left him in little doubt that they had obtained the 'just cause' required for a full trial.

Sure enough, once the court had reconvened and all were seated, Judge Franco made his statement. "Having listened to the case on both sides, despite the accused plea of not guilty, we find sufficient contents here this morning to justify setting a trial date. It will be for six weeks hence on the 27th of next month."

Sergio's lawyer then requested bail for his client. The judge stated that due to the seriousness of the case, bail would not be granted.

With that, the courtroom was cleared and Sergio was taken back into police custody.

All today had gone as the prosecution had wanted.

Chapter 39

During the six weeks before the formal trial date, a lot happened at Pathways.

Four of the recruited team left to start new ventures elsewhere. Peter left to attend his interview in Poole, Dorset, and just a week after leaving, he called Antonio and told him that he had successfully got the position there and had started straight away. He again thanked Antonio for all his help to assist this fresh start. He was truly grateful. Michael and Joanna departed for a new life in Las Vegas. They were rather emotional when the day to leave came but they were clearly excited at this new chapter in their lives together. Angela left too. She took her one-way flight to Glasgow where she planned to resume her singing career at one or more of the many nightclubs there.

Jonathan had now opened his boxing school at the snooker club and quite quickly enrolled his first students. It looked as though this was going to be a successful venture and was therefore a good decision.

This just left Wan and George with, as yet, no work or project to become involved with, but were ready now to discuss their plan for acquiring the casino with Antonio and Kokee. They took their moment a week after the others had left and all was quiet at the hotel. They set up a formal meeting one afternoon with them both.

They proposed that, together with them, they make a low offer to purchase the casino on a three-share basis. They had already had the empty casino valued and their proposed offer was to be thirty per cent below that, as a starting point. Their proposal was that Antonio would only be required for advice and the initial setting up of everything. After that, Wan explained that he and George would manage everything from then on. Ownership and earnings would be on a three-way basis. They went on to say that they didn't realistically expect to achieve the purchase at that price, but that this offer would likely get a good deal not far off that figure eventually.

Antonio told them that this was certainly a possibility for him but such a bold forward move involving substantial capital needed some thought. He told them that he and Kokee would consider this plan and have a decision within a few days. Both Wan and George were well content with this reaction. It was certainly not the negative response they could have received.

It would be true to say that he and Kokee were feeling content with the way all was going. The main thing for Antonio was to see Kokee gaining strength daily. She surely would now regain full mobility and a complete recovery from the pain she initially had suffered.

The children's little school was working perfectly and Kokee was really enjoying her new work of helping these children. They certainly seemed to have taken her to their hearts. In fact, the school had now moved to five mornings a week, rather than just the three it operated before. It was another success story.

To complete the relaxed feeling that Antonio was experiencing, he was certain now that Sergio at least would be convicted and imprisoned within just a few days hence now.

Life was certainly moving forward positively for this lovely couple. They both felt that Karma was doing its thing for them at last. But would it turn out how they hoped and expected, that was the question.

There was perhaps a long way yet to go…

Chapter 40

The day before the full trial was to start, everyone there had a surprise! Michael and Joanna arrived back from Las Vegas to visit. Michael explained that their visit was two-fold. Firstly, they wanted to offer their support to Antonio and Kokee during this trial, and secondly, Michael wanted to see how his dad was getting on now he was on his own for the first time in a long while. It was clear that everyone was pleased to see them return.

The trial was called to a session at 9.30 am prompt the following morning as scheduled. The prosecution addressed the judges and of course, the whole court, which was crowded with spectators. Antonio and Kokee were so well-known and popular, that a sizeable turnout such as this had been expected.

He went through the whole case against Sergio, the charge being the attempted murder of Antonio. He described what had happened that day in graphic detail. He pulled no punches in recounting everything that had transpired, including the hiding of evidence—the rifle, the exhaust on the getaway car, and finally, the offending bullet.

During the whole of this first day, witnesses were called and questioned by both sides.

First to be called was Diego, who was the person at the back of the group on that afternoon. He was asked to describe what he had heard and seen. He explained, "I heard a crack, rather like a gunshot, and turned around to see where it had come from. In doing so, I saw one or possibly two men scampering into a small white car, which then sped away at speed making a very loud noise."

"What did you think the unusual sound coming from the car was?" The prosecutor asked.

"I was sure it was a leaking exhaust system," he replied. "Then, I looked forward again to see Kokee on the floor and concluded she had been shot." The prosecutor thanked him and sat down.

The defence lawyer first asked if he could describe the person getting into the car. He replied that he was not able to do this with any certainty. "Are you sure the car was white? After all, it was apparently a long way away, wasn't it? I put it to you that it could have been grey or even light blue."

He replied, "No, it was definitely white." The prosecutor then asked if he took note of its registration details. The witness could only say that it was sideways onto him and too far away to do this.

After that, the defence lawyer said he had no further questions; they both sat down.

Next to be called was Hugo Garcia. He was the person who had reported hearing a conversation about a rifle in the restaurant.

"Tell us what you saw and heard that evening," the prosecutor said.

The witness replied, "There was a conversation between a diner and the restaurant owner about a rifle and ammunition that had been kept in the restaurant. The restaurant owner said that he wanted them to be taken away urgently. Then shortly after, I saw the diner walk away carrying a bulky bag over his shoulder."

"Could you identify or describe this person?"

"Unfortunately, I cannot be much help here as he had his back to me and was on the other side of the restaurant, by the door. I can say, however, that he was dark-haired, slim, and of more than average height."

The defence lawyer asked the next question. "Did anyone else hear this supposed conversation?"

"No," he replied. "It was early and nobody else was there."

"So, we have just your word that this happened and in any case, you are not able to identify this person, nor really even able to describe him?" The witness had to agree with this.

The young assistant working in the sports shop was the next to take the stand. All he was able to do was to confirm they had sold some ammunition to someone who was at least similar to the accused and that it was for the rifle type later found in Sergio's possession. The defence then asked, "Could you be certain, beyond any doubt, that that person was the accused sitting before us here today?"

"No, not with total certainty," he replied.

The penultimate witness for the day was the garage owner who had fitted the new exhaust to Sergio's white car. He was asked to confirm that he had indeed fitted this to his car the very day following the shooting. He was able to do that but added a vital piece of information. He told the court, "Sergio insisted it was urgent and needed to be fitted that day because he had been stopped and warned by the police to cease using the vehicle immediately."

The defence offered no questions for this witness.

The final witness was the senior police inspector for the region. He was asked if he could confirm that Sergio had indeed been stopped and warned about this noisy exhaust as had been claimed. He promptly stated that there was no record of this ever having happened. There were gasps around the court at this piece of evidence that seemed to show Sergio to be a liar.

The prosecuting lawyer then asked, "Can you please tell us what happened when your officer went to the hospital to collect the bullet that had been removed from Kokee as had been arranged?"

"Yes, I can. When he arrived, he was told that it had already been collected by someone else earlier. We knew this wasn't one of our officers, so we asked to see the CCTV recording made by the security camera in this reception area. We have it here for the court to see."

The judge requested it to be played and to be frame frozen at the point where the man collecting the package could be seen. When this was done, all could clearly identify this person as Sergio, sitting in the dock!

The court went into an uproar. Judge Franco banged his gavel on the table and demanded silence. He then adjourned the court and asked everyone to return at 9.30 am the following day.

Antonio and Kokee met in private with their lawyer for a debrief after this opening day. He told them that he felt a large amount of evidence, albeit mostly circumstantial, was well received by the judges and that he felt it had been very difficult for the defence to come up with anything original to contradict what had been submitted. Whilst this was true, the question was, would it be enough to prove guilt without any reasonable doubt?

That evening, the atmosphere in the hotel was a little uneasy and conversations were few and little was said about the case. Instead, the weather and the current basketball game at the local stadium were mainly the discussion topics. Perhaps, this was a nervous reaction to the real goings-on. Michael enjoyed a catch-up with his dad, who told him all about his boxing club at the snooker hall. He was so happy to see him settled into a project to keep him busy and hopefully to make him a living.

The mayor visited Antonio that evening and apologised for not being able to attend the first day of this all-important trial. He did, however, promise to be there for the next day. They had dinner together.

Lola, the owner of the children's school was, unknown to Kokee, in the visitors' gallery that day. She had made a good friendship with her and came to offer her support. She came over and talked with Kokee after dinner. This gave further encouragement for her to see this right the way through. This lovely couple had so much support and the right was clearly on their side. But could the right decision come at the end of the trauma they had all been through?

Chapter 41

The court was called into session by the judges, not at 9.30 as scheduled, but for some inexplicable reason delayed to 10.15. All had waited patiently for the judges to arrive. When they did, no apology or explanation was offered. Judges seem to think themselves all-powerful and feel they have no need to explain themselves to anyone in Guatemala.

After calling the court to order, the prosecution made its final summing up.

They clearly outlined what they believed had happened. They also explained the motive behind the murder attempt; namely, the disputes over the casino. By the time he stood down, few had any doubts as to the guilt of the accused. But would the judges see it that way too?

Then, it was the job of the defence. They outlined their case which simply kept harping back to the circumstantial nature of all the evidence. Each witness stood firmly to their statements, refuting all the prosecution had put forward as fact. Their lawyer faced the judges and stood very close to them as he made his final statement.

He said, "Can you honestly say that you have heard even a single piece of evidence that is unshakeable proof of this charge, anything that is more than opinion? I put it to you, there is nothing to find my client guilty without any reasonable doubt. This fantasy case must be surely dismissed." With that, he sat down.

The judges announced that they would adjourn to deliberate and consider carefully all they had heard. They requested all to return for their final decision at 2 pm the following afternoon. All then left the courtroom.

That evening, there were lively conversations around Pathways. Emotions were running high with anticipation.

Jonathan took his son and Joanna to the snooker club they both knew well, not to play but to show off his new boxing school. Michael was sincerely impressed with what his father had done and told him so. He had worried about his dad, left behind, but could see he needn't have done so. He was clearly content with what he was doing.

Wan and George secretly had purchased, at some considerable cost, a magnum of Moet & Chandon quality French champagne and had it on ice, hidden away ready for what they hoped would be a celebration the following evening.

Antonio's brother, Carlos, had an uneasy conversation with him when approached. He didn't give the impression that he had sympathy for Kokee or him at all. More than that, he just wanted to see this trial conclude. Antonio felt his stance and body language were strange. Neither he nor Kokee could make much sense of it when discussing it later as they turned in for the night.

It was probably true to say that few were able to sleep a normal relaxed night. Too much was going around in so many people's minds for that.

Chapter 42
Final Chapter

Well before 2 pm, all were seated in the courtroom and eager for the conclusion to this emotive case. A few minutes after 2 pm, the same three judges appeared and called the court into session. Judge Franco stood and called all to order.

After asking Sergio to stand, he explained that this had been a complicated case and a difficult decision for them to arrive at. He explained why.

"In cases where the evidence is largely circumstantial, a conviction is usually unlikely. In this case, it is true that this is what we have faced, but the difference here is that there is just so much of it. Weighing it all up, we therefore have no uncertainty as to the guilt of the accused and we find this charge proven without any reasonable doubt."

Sighs of relief ran around the room. He went on, "We hereby sentence you to a term of imprisonment to be fifteen years, without parole. You have the right to appeal this decision." There was some applause at this but Judge Franco swiftly quelled it. Then, a shocking and most unexpected thing happened.

Sergio shouted out, pointing at Antonio's brother, Carlos.

"He is the person who should be standing here. Yes, I took the shot but it was his plan from beginning to end. He bought the rifle and gave it to me. He also paid me to take the shot that afternoon." He had more to say.

"How do you think I knew the exact details of the party that afternoon and how did I know exactly when, where, and how I could collect the bullet? Carlos gave me all that information."

Carlos stood, looking shaken and pale, and attempted to leave the courtroom, but was swiftly stopped by two officers standing guard at the rear. Antonio too leapt to his feet and shouted, "Bastardo, Bastardo!" He then aggressively attempted to get to Carlos but was quickly restrained by the court security guards.

Sergio was taken down to start his jail term, Carlos was taken to the police station for questioning, and the court dispersed.

Carlos, eventually, said he did it because he was angry Antonio had left him to run the plantation alone and also that he was still sore from not being chosen as Antonio's best man. He clearly had become a very bitter person.

Back at the hotel, there was much relief at Sergio's conviction, but the celebrations that naturally followed were somewhat dampened by the shocking revelation that Antonio's brother was responsible for this wicked act.

Antonio and Kokee were stunned, confused, but above all, angry at what had just been revealed. To realise that his own brother was responsible for the loss of their baby was just too much to fully take in. They both retired to their rooms, not now feeling like any kind of celebration.

They discussed Carlos and his actions and began to realise that the original problems with the brothers and their casinos were probably all down to him from the very beginning. He was most likely responsible for it all.

Back in the bar, the champagne was opened and enjoyed by the others.

At the police station, Carlos was charged with conspiring to attempt a murder. He made a full confession as he realistically had little other option. In the fullness of time, he too would be sent to prison for a lengthy term, possibly a longer one than Sergio had received.

Now, it was time for everyone to try to put the past behind them and get on with their lives. This was exactly what they all did, some found this easier than others. Certainly, Antonio and Kokee's mental wounds would take a considerable time to heal.

During the following months, things at Pathways did return to something more like normality.

The only website it now had was as a restaurant and hotel; happiness returned and some truly wonderful things followed.

Together with Antonio, Wan and George bought the casino and month by month, they made it ever more successful. Antonio's role was only as an advisor, not being interested in the day-to-day running of it.

Having quite quickly succeeded in signing up members for his boxing school, Michael made it into a most profitable venture and really enjoyed his work there.

After several rejected attempts, Lola finally succeeded in getting the local authority to reinstate the grant she had lost. Using this most welcome funding, she was able to lease a larger facility to expand her school, which was rapidly outgrowing the space that had been kindly lent to her at Pathways.

Kokee continued to assist Lola with the education of the children on a part-time voluntary basis. This was something she really enjoyed doing, she didn't consider it to be work in any way.

After a little over five months passed, Kokee announced that she was three months pregnant and was expecting a baby boy again. This wonderful news was greeted with great excitement by all who knew them. Everyone hoped this would bring them the happiness they knew they now deserved.

So, some stories can be sad and some pathways can be most difficult to travel, but thankfully, many do finally have happy endings.

THE END